Sins of a
Side Chick

Sins of a Side Chick

Kandie Marie

www.urbanbooks.net

Urban Books, LLC
300 Farmingdale Road, N.Y.-Route 109
Farmingdale, NY 11735

ISBN 13: 978-1-64556-727-1
EBOOK ISBN: 978-1-64556-739-4

First Trade Paperback Printing October 2025
Printed in the United States of America

10 9 8 7 6 5 4 3 2 1

Distributed by Kensington Publishing Corp.
Submit Orders to:
Customer Service
400 Hahn Road
Westminster, MD 21157-4627
Phone: 1-800-733-3000
Fax: 1-800-659-2436

The authorized representative in the EU for product safety and compliance
Is eucomply OÜ, Parnu mnt 139b-14, Apt 123
Tallinn, Berlin 11317, hello@eucompliancepartner.com

Acknowledgments

As always, I have to thank God on high for giving me this talent and always being here for me.

This book is dedicated to my heart, Robert L. Pope, who passed away while I was writing this book. As I continue to grieve and work through life without him, I'm pushing through, and I know you are looking down at us and are so proud.

This book is also dedicated to my son, who gives me all the strength and power in the world. Jayveion, I love you and thank you for being the best gift I could've ever been blessed with.

Last but never least, to each and every one of my readers, you all are so amazing and have been so supportive. I just want to thank you guys for rocking with me. I promise I'm not done yet. I hope I made you all proud.

Dear Diary,

It's March 20, 2016, and you know what today is? It's my motherfucking birthday. I'm officially 21 years old, legal to do all things! I awoke this morning in the best way. My bae, Eric, woke me up the best way a girl could imagine. So, let me tell you what happened.

I was in a deep sleep, completely exhausted from work and step practice from the previous night. Awaking me, Eric pulled the covers off my half-naked body, allowing the cool breeze from the ceiling fan to hit my round, chocolate ass. Opening my eyes slightly, I saw him staring at me in awe.

I asked him, "What are you doing? I'm cold, nigga. Give me the damn blanket."

"It's your birthday, babe. I wanna give you the first present of the day," he whispered, leaning over to nibble on my ear.

"Eric, it's what? Like four in the morning? It can wait, babe. Let's just go back to sleep," I pleaded with him, trying to pull the covers back over me.

Let me tell you, bae wasn't having it. He yanked the crimson jersey knit sheets off me again. I opened my eyes, looking at his beautiful, bronzed skin, all of his tattoos covering his chest, and those dark brown eyes peering through my soul, and it made it hard for me to say no.

He lowered his body to the edge of our queen-sized bed, then looked up at me and said, "You are so beautiful."

Pushing my legs apart, he slowly stuck his tongue into my pussy hole. I let out a gasp as I held on to the sheets. His tongue penetrated my pussy over and over, and then he moved his tongue from my pussy hole, placing his whole mouth on my clit. My moans aroused him, making him suck harder on my pussy. I gyrated my hips against his face as I felt myself about to explode. When he tried to lift his head for air, I shoved it back down, moaning, "Don't stop."

His mouth was doing wonders for me, and I loved every minute. The moment my legs lost their grip around his neck, quivering from the climax, he got up and kneeled on the bed, both of us panting like dogs in heat.

Sitting up, I leaned over, reaching for his boxers and pulling them down to let his thick, long-ass ten-inch cock burst out. I grabbed it and caressed it slowly. He was as hard as a rock before I even placed my lips on the tip of his dick.

"Mmm, tell me what you want, daddy," I stated seductively while I groped him.

"It's whatever you want to do, baby," he replied lowly, looking down at me.

I smirked. "Mmm, well, I want to do this." Opening my mouth as wide as I could and placing my wet mouth around the head of his dick, I started sucking it slowly. Eric grabbed my hair as he let out a slight moan. But I was just getting started. I slid my mouth lower onto his dick, attempting to swallow all ten inches until he hit my tonsils.

"*Fuck,*" *he moaned loudly as he held my head right at the base of his shaft. "I'm about to fuck your face, you hear me?" he asked as he thrust his dick back and forth in my mouth.*

The taste of him, hearing his moans, and his gripping my hair excited me. I started rubbing on my clit, making sure she stayed ready for him. He fucked my face until I began to gag, which made us both hornier. When I took his dick out of my mouth, I was ready to fuck.

"Give me that dick, daddy. I want it," I said, insisting that he fuck me after all that foreplay, but to my surprise, he disappointed me.

"Not yet, baby. Daddy has some other things in store for you today. You just gonna have to wait a little," he teased while rubbing the tip on my pussy.

"Well, just a little sample of what I will get later?" I inquired, pulling my T-shirt over my head, leaving nothing on me but the charm bracelet from Pandora he got me for Christmas.

He couldn't resist, and neither could I. "Just a taste," he said as he slid inside me. He lifted my right leg, placing it around his neck, as he stroked deep inside of me, filling me up, literally. I dug my nails from my left hand into his left arm as he gripped the sheets, pumping his dick into me.

His pace quickened, and then, dropping my leg back down, he shoved one of my 38-D breasts into his mouth. As he sucked and nibbled on my tit, his dick was digging into my pussy like it was searching for a pot of gold.

My pussy pulsated and gripped his dick, and his stroke got harder, faster. I knew it wouldn't be long before I would come.

"Yeah, that's it. Give daddy that cum. Come for daddy, you nasty, little bitch," he moaned, kneeling up again and pushing my legs all the way back to our windowsill.

"Daddy, daddy," I yelled.

"Fuck, yes, baby. Fuckkkk," he shrieked in pleasure as we came together.

His nut filled my pussy, and I didn't care. As long as we had been together, there was no reason why he shouldn't nut in me, you know? Eric lay on top of me, trying to catch his breath.

"You just couldn't wait, huh?" he joked.

"Well, I'm sure there will be plenty more rounds later," I replied, snickering while running my fingers down his back.

Honestly, I wanted more of him. Shit, I needed more of him. But he wanted me to wait.

He was so perfect. We are so perfect for each other and to each other that it's crazy. He fulfills me sexually, mentally, and emotionally. He's the perfect man, and I felt lucky to have had him this long. Lord knows, his mom did a bomb-ass job raising him.

Eric left me in bed around eight this morning, telling me to prepare for an amazing twenty-first. If the rest of the day will be anything like this morning, I know it will be well worth the wait. Diary, I'll get back to you in a bit.

Reneece

Chapter 1

Reneece

Later That Day

I finally got out of our bed around eleven to Eric yelling at the top of his lungs. "Reneece, bring yo' ass here, girl," he said. "Babe, come on, get down here."

Rising out of the bed, I noticed a wet spot in the middle of it from our little sexcape from that morning. I grabbed my scrunchie from our wooden nightstand, throwing my medium-length honey-blond hair into a high ponytail as I removed the sheets from the bed. Eric continued hollering for me to come downstairs, but I had to change those sheets first.

"I'm coming, babe, damn," I shouted out of the bedroom. I felt myself becoming irritated at him.

I heard him let out a slight laugh, then mumble, "Not fast enough," as he walked away from the bottom of the steps. As I changed the bed, the aroma of freshly cooked bacon, pancakes, and even scrambled eggs filled our home. Scurrying to brush my teeth to get to those smells, I thought, *This man has made me breakfast, plus gave me some bomb-ass dick. This is going to be a great birthday, after all.*

After getting my hygiene and appearance together, I ran down the steps, ready to eat and see what he was bellowing about. There, scattered all over my red, faux fur rug, he had twenty-one gifts laid out.

"What's all this?" I asked, shocked, as I approached the living room.

He grabbed me by the hand and led me to the couch. "Happy birthday, beautiful."

I looked into his eyes. "Babe, all of this . . . This is for me?"

With a slight chuckle and nod, he responded, "Yeah, babe, you definitely deserve it."

Eric stood before me and leaned over to give me a simple, sweet kiss on my cheek before entering the kitchen.

"Before opening your presents, you should eat something first." He returned with a brown tray; on top of it, a paper plate was filled with cheese grits, two pancakes, scrambled eggs, and bacon.

"Okay, either you're being super nice, you up to something, or you fucked up. 'Cause you never cook, at least like this." Reaching for the tray, I joked with him.

"Well, it's your birthday, plus, I know you been feeling like I been distant. I want you to know that I love you, and there's nothing and no one else I would rather be with," he said while walking toward the front door.

"Nigga, where you going?" I questioned, noticing him put on his Nike slides.

"I'll be right back. I have a quick errand to run. I don't want anything interrupting us today. So eat. Open your presents like it's Christmas and shit, and I'll be back before you know it." Then returning to the couch, he pinched my cheek and stole one of my slices of bacon before heading out the door.

I know some women would've been bothered, but with all the clubs he was in, plus his frat, I'm sure he just wanted to take care of those things so they wouldn't be calling and shit. Lord knows I hated when we had a date night or something, and he would have to run to a meeting or an event. As he walked out the door, I sat on our couch, looking like a little kid on Christmas with all these gifts in front of me, ready to dig into each one.

Eagerly pulling the first box toward me, I noticed it was wrapped up so well, covered in a cream-colored wrapping paper, and tied in a gold bow. It was so beautiful to look at that I almost didn't want to open it. I gently pulled on the satin ribbon, letting it fall into my lap, then tore off the wrapping paper to find a pair of black stilettos inside with a twenty-dollar bill stuffed inside each shoe.

Stuffing the money into my bra and placing the stilettos on the floor beside me, I moved off the couch to grab a medium-sized brown gift bag with the words *"Birthday Princess"* written on the front. The bag wasn't too heavy, and an envelope lay on the top. When I opened the envelope, I found a birthday card with forty dollars inside of it. The card was simple, but what he wrote inside melted my heart.

> *To my beautiful girlfriend, Reneece,*
> *I hope these gifts show you how much you mean to me. I hope everything fits. I just wanna thank you for being an awesome girlfriend and my best friend. I love you, baby. I have a bigger surprise for you later. You can open the other gifts later, but go ahead and open the one in the rectangular box near the TV. I'll see you later, babe.*
> *Eric*

The card was sweet, especially for a man who wasn't super vocal about his emotions or feelings. Sometimes, I wondered if he loved me or at least was still in love with me after all this time. Being with someone since high school and growing up with them daily is something serious. It's hard sometimes, I can't lie.

Placing the bag on our suede black sofa next to my uneaten plate of food, I stood up and walked over to the TV. Just like Eric said, beside it was a long rectangular box with the same wrapping paper, but this time, a black ribbon. I bent over to detach the small note that dangled from the ribbon.

I can't wait to see you wear this tonight, it read. I assumed the inside of the box was lingerie, so I took the box and the heels he bought me upstairs so I could try them on in my full-length mirror. Laying the box on the bed, I opened it and was pleasantly surprised. Inside was a beautiful, red satin, strapless dress with a heart shape cut at the top. It draped low in the back. I couldn't wait to see how it would fit. Underneath the dress was a black lingerie teddy piece. It was completely lace, with garter straps around the legs.

At that moment, I was feeling myself. I began undressing so I could take a shower before Eric got home. I was about to show him how much I appreciated all the gifts and the time he put into making my birthday memorable.

Knock, knock, knock.

I heard the knocking as I was about to go into the bathroom. I tried to ignore it, thinking it maybe was a Jehovah's Witness or something. Running my bathwater, I could hear the knocks get louder. Completely irritated now, I grabbed my big, lavender towel, wrapped it around my naked body, and ran down the stairs to see who it was.

Yelling "Hold on" so they would stop knocking, I finally reached the last step. Before I even opened my door, I looked through the peephole to see who it was. There, standing in front of the door and banging on it, was some rat-faced-looking bitch. You know, like that nigga off of the wire, only uglier. I opened the door just slightly to see if maybe she was lost, and things immediately took a wrong turn.

"Yo' name Renee?" she asked while attempting to push my door back.

"No, my name is Reneece, and maybe you have the wrong house," I stated, pushing my door shut.

She grabbed the door before I could shut it completely. "I'm looking for Eric," she said.

She piqued my interest when she said my nigga's name. "Why are you looking for him?"

"I have something to tell him," she responded cynically.

"Whatever you need to tell him, you can tell me," I retorted, pulling the door back, then folding my arms across my chest.

"No, I want, and I *need,* to tell him personally, not through a third party," she countered as she reached into her pocket, pulling out a melted piece of gum.

"And that would be *what* exactly?" I inquired, watching her chew the gum with her mouth wide open, showing her missing teeth on the side. I almost threw up watching the spectacle.

She laughed in my face with spit flying everywhere. "Tell him Dareen stopped by," she said, throwing up her middle finger at me as she walked to the parking lot.

Eric never mentioned anyone named Dareen before, and for her to have the balls to come to my house, especially on *my* birthday, made me fucking livid *and* intrigued to know what the hell she wanted to tell him. My intuition was telling me there was some bullshit about to come my way.

After she left, I couldn't take my mind off that purple-black, rat-toothed-face, Whoopi Goldberg look-alike. I called Eric for a good thirty minutes straight and received no answer. The more my calls went unanswered, the more curious, angrier, and baffled I got by the second. Two hours later, guess who finally arrived home?

It was about six o'clock that evening when Eric walked in. He came in the door, turning on the tall lamp, to find me on the couch, my arms folded and a stone-cold face. He looked at me, confused, not sure what was wrong.

"Hey, babe," he said, walking over, attempting to kiss me, but I wasn't here for it.

Shoving him away from me, I shouted, "Don't you 'Hey fucking babe me.' I know you saw me fucking calling you. Why didn't you answer? Were you *that* busy you couldn't answer my calls or text me?"

He stepped back into the middle of the living room floor. "What's wrong? Did you not like your gifts?"

I was so enraged at that point that I threw one of the unopened gift boxes at him, yelling, "This isn't about no damn presents! You know why I'm upset. Stop playing fucking dumb."

In my mind, I knew that that ugly-ass bitch probably called him. I don't get why he's acting so fucking confused.

He approached me cautiously and asked, "So, what's the issue? I can't do nothing to surprise you?"

"Who the fuck is she?" I uttered.

His eyes widened. "Who?"

Taking a deep breath, I clenched my hands together before I went off. "Don't you dare sit here and play dumb with me. Who the fuck is she, Eric?"

He looked surprised, still playing dumb. "Babe, I seriously have no clue what you're talking about."

"Dareen. Who the fuck is Dareen? Answer me now, Eric," I demanded, walking up to him with my fists balled up, ready to punch him in his shit if he was going to deny knowing her.

He just stood there silent, dumbfounded, as if he was looking for something to say or how to answer me.

"Eric, you not going to say shit?" Using the back of my left hand to slap him across his face, I had to ask the lingering question. "You fucking her? You fucked her in *my* house?"

"Babe, listen," he said.

"Nah, motherfucker, answer my question."

He fell to his knees, grabbing and caressing my legs. Tears leaked down his face. He just kept saying he was sorry. That's all he would say . . . over, and over, and fucking over. "I'm sorry."

"How long you been fucking her?" I asked in a whisper.

"It was just a few times, and I . . ." He clung to my legs, refusing to let me move.

Kneeing him in his chest, I asked him again. "How long, Eric? More importantly, how the fuck did she know where I stayed?"

Since he didn't respond, I asked, "Did you fuck her in our home? In our *bed?*"

He still didn't respond. I pulled away from him. I couldn't believe not only had he cheated on me, but he also did the ultimate disrespect by having her in a home that we shared. This nigga has truly lost his fucking mind. I hit him with whatever was nearby and then said, "Hey, aye, are you serious? You can't be serious. Not only were you cheating with a gorilla, but you also fucked her in my shit?"

"I fucked up," he said, looking up at me like a sad puppy dog.

"Yeah, you damn right you fucked up." Shoving him out of my way, I headed toward the stairs in utter disgust.

"I'm sorry, Reneece. Baby, I'm sorry," he yelled, following behind me.

I walked into my bedroom, and when I looked at my bed, I could envision all the times he probably fucked her there—on *my* sheets. The way he probably kissed her, even if he ate her pussy, or how she probably tried to swallow his dick like it was a hot dog or some shit. As the tears ran down my eyes, I started to throw all the sheets and covers off the bed. Then I grabbed his clothes and started throwing them down the stairs.

"Reneece, what the fuck?"

"Get the fuck out."

"Come on, can we talk about this?"

"You can't be serious."

"Come on, it's your birthday. I can make this right. Please, let me try."

As I cried, I began to laugh. I was either losing my mind, or I was trying to refrain from killing him. I couldn't get those images out of my mind.

"Fuck you, Eric. Fuck you."

"Babe—"

"Fuck you. Fuck my birthday. I hope your fucking balls and dick fall off, you piece of shit."

Eric tried to walk up the stairs as I threw his sneakers at him, yelling at him to get out of my house. I needed my space and time to digest all of this. Standing there, he just looked at me, full of regret, taking the hits and weeping like a bitch. It almost seemed like he was crying more than I was.

"I'm not fucking leaving, so keep throwing shit. I'm *not* fucking leaving," he declared.

"I'll call the police if you don't leave," I shouted so he would understand that it was time for some space.

"You're overreacting right now," he murmured.

"Eric, you cheated on me and had the audacity to sleep with the ho in my fucking house. What the hell do you mean? If it was the other way around, no telling how you'd be acting, so fuck you. Don't you fucking dare tell me that I'm overreacting or how to feel right now," I said before balling up my fist, then punching the wall to the right of me.

Eric started to walk down the stairs. Then he looked at me and said, "After six years . . . We been together *six* years."

"You should've remembered that when you stuck your dick in that raggedy ho," I yelled at him with my back turned.

I walked back into my room and slammed the door. I couldn't believe he did this to me—to *us*. I gave him all of me in so many ways. All the time, energy, love—all of it, I put into him, into us. And *this* is how he fucking repaid me? He doesn't love me. How could he? I made him my first love, I let him make me into a woman. And now, here I am.

As I continued to scream I hated him, Eric was banging on the bedroom door, begging me to let him in. He constantly groaned, "I'm sorry," but I wasn't hearing it. I knew if he didn't leave, I needed to. I grabbed whatever I needed in eyesight and packed a quick overnight bag before storming out of the bedroom. I wasn't sure where I was going at that moment, but I just knew I was leaving.

"Move out of my way," I demanded.

"Baby, please. I wanna fix this—fix us. It's your birthday. I planned something special for you tonight," he pleaded.

Attempting to walk past him, I said, "Eric, move out of my way," as he tried to grab my hand.

"Reneece," he called, begging me to stay.

"Eric, I said move—damn." I pushed my way out of his path and knocked him into one of the mirrors adjacent to the rail on the stairs.

My emotions were all over the place. I didn't realize I had shoved him into the wall as hard as I did. His head was bleeding slightly. I wanted to nurse it, but I needed to leave. I turned back to look one last time before running out the door to my car. I left him there with everything and headed to Jalisa's house, my girl, to clear my mind.

Dear Diary,

I can't believe this shit is happening to me. I departed from what used to be our home and drove to Jalisa's. Had I stayed there another minute, there was no telling what could have happened because he just wouldn't let me leave.

Diary, if you could've been a fly on the wall, you know these past few hours have been hell. Everything was cool at first. I went through my presents, then suddenly, a random knock came to my door. I wasn't gonna answer it at first, but I'm glad I did. A girl named Dareen came asking me for Eric. Like that rat-face bitch had a whole lot of balls, let alone the audacity, to go to my home. This shit there was unbelievable. When I confronted Eric, he decided to play stupid. Ugh. I hate him. I fucking hate him. I hate him for making me believe he loved me. I hate him for making me his fool and thinking he was the perfect fucking man.

Here I am, sitting in Jalisa's parking lot, uncontrollably crying. I'm hurt. No, I'm way beyond hurt. I hope they are fucking happy together. I'm done with his ass. See, that's what's wrong with niggas. They always wanna use the smallest fuckin' reason, or at times, no reason at all, but they'll go fuck the first bitch they see. But she will never amount to half the woman I am.

I may not be the baddest bitch, but I sometimes like thinking of myself as being a thicker version of Kelly Rowland with my medium-length natural honey-blond hair, beautiful brown eyes, cute feet, educated look, and streetwise. I'm one hell of a catch. I refuse to let him or any man make me feel otherwise.

Come to think of it, I've seen that ho around before. I think she fucked my line sister's nigga last year. Things between them were always so messed up, but she called me late one night. If so, Rat Face ain't nothing but a ho. And that's what he likes? I wish he would just stop calling me. I don't want to talk. There's nothing to talk about. He can never fix this. Men don't understand how they damage us with the little lies they tell. The cheating. The flirting. Do you understand?

Eric would've flipped his lid if he ever thought I fucked another nigga. I should go fuck someone just for the hell of it. He doesn't understand how much fucking dick I could've been riding the fuck out of had I only known that he was out here doing him.

I think it's best if I let him have the apartment and I stay with my girl Jalisa for a while. I need time to think and figure things out. Going to my sisters would not be the business. Knowing them, they wouldn't do anything but make matters worse. I don't think I will ever be able to love again, let alone be in another relationship. But I guess I should go in. I can see Jalisa eyeing me from her steps, and if I continue to sit in this car, she'll come get me. I'll catch up with you later.

Reneece

Chapter 2

Dareen

Walking into my dorm building, New Baynes, I could feel my phone vibrating relentlessly. Now this nigga wants to call me. I guess his ugly-ass girlfriend told him I stopped by. Well, when I wanted to talk, he ignored my calls and texts. Even when I popped up to his meetings and practices, he proceeded with life as if he didn't know me. For the past ten months, Eric and I been knocking boots all over campus whenever we could. I knew he was talking to someone, but I didn't know how serious they were 'til I went out for the Delta line earlier this year.

My name is Dareen. I'm a beautiful chocolate goddess. I got around on campus, but not in that way. I thought all these guys wanted something serious with me, but I wouldn't hear from them again after a few weeks. Things with Eric were so different. I remember the night I met him, like yesterday, about a year ago. He had been sweating me that whole month in class, always trying to sit next to me, but word was that he had a girlfriend, so I wouldn't give him any of my time.

This one night in particular, me and this girl I became cool with, Royal, went out to this frat house party. We stopped at a nearby liquor store near Northgate Mall to grab our own bottles. The thing with frat parties is that their drinks, or should I say, "party juice," would have you gone after one cup, so to refrain from anything crazy happening to us, we decided to have our own alcohol handy.

We arrived a little after midnight, and everyone seemed just to be getting there. There were barely any nearby parking spaces, so we parked farther down the street. Royal always seemed to get the best dudes to talk to her, and it sometimes made me a little jealous.

I watched her apply her purple lipstick on her pink lips with her high-yellow ass. Rolling my eyes and turning my head out the window, I noticed Eric walking down to the two-story brick house where everyone was lingering around.

"Girl, don't you think you got enough of that shit on?" I asked, ready to get out of the car.

"What's the rush? Ain't like you checkin' for anyone or anyone checkin' for you," she replied conceitedly while puckering her lips up like a duck.

"You know what? Fuck you, all right. Let's just go." I got out of the car, slamming the door behind me. I was halfway to the house when Royal caught up to me.

"You look cute, girl," she said, pulling on my skirt.

"It was something last minute I just pulled out." Brushing off her compliment, I took my bottle of pineapple Amsterdam vodka out of my bag.

My outfit that night was mad cute, though. I wore an attractive black miniskirt that fit tight enough for my ass to really poke out, my white *I Love NCCU* shirt that I made into a crop top, with my white Converse. Sometimes, simple can be just as cute. Now, Royal was out here looking like a straight diva. With her patent leather purple heels, white with purple polka-dots strapless dress, and her hair up in a high bun, you would think she was going to the club, not someone's whack-ass house party.

When we walked in, everyone stopped to hug her or acknowledge her presence in some way. I had no clue Royal knew all them people, but I guess since she was a cheerleader, she was known somehow.

As we made our way through the crowd, the music was jumping. The "Nasty Song" was blasting through the speakers. Around every corner, niggas were getting they dicks grinded on. We were halfway to the living area when I looked back, noticing Royal had been snatched up. She was bent over, ass tooted in the air, while she shook her ass on this tall, heavyset dude.

Turning back to get to my only friend there, I felt someone touch my shoulder.

"I didn't know you partied," he screamed over the music in my ear.

Turning around to see who it was, to my surprise, I found out it was Eric. "Not that often. I'm usually in my dorm."

"You wanna dance?" he asked before sipping from his red plastic cup.

"Nah, I don't dance." I gracefully declined his offer.

"Come on. It'll be fun," he said, taking my hand and leading me into the middle of the living room floor.

Pulling my bottle back out of my bag, I took another swig and thought, *What the hell.* The song was ending when "Back That Azz" up started to play. Now, I wasn't that good at shaking my ass, but with a bit of liquor, I loosened up.

He bent me over as he thrust against me while I attempted to twerk. I was probably looking crazy to some people and maybe him. After a good five minutes, I was over it and stood back up.

Following me to a nearby green lawn chair, he sat and conversed with me throughout the party, never leaving my side. He made me feel so comfortable and desired, more than any nigga I had dealt with in the past. It was getting late now; people were leaving little by little.

He sat me on his lap, where I could feel his hardened cock trying to break free. From what I could feel, it was a decent size. I didn't know if it was the liquor or if I was just that horny, but I asked him if he wanted to take me back to campus. I thought he would've said no, but he tapped my legs, motioning that he was ready to leave too.

As we walked to his car, his phone was in his hand, vibrating like crazy. The first few times, he let it ring, but when the calls wouldn't stop, he turned it off.

"Who's that blowing you up?" I inquired, trying to see who would be callin' him like that.

"It's some crazy ex. You know how some girls can be. Don't know how to let things be over," he responded as we reached his all-black Dodge Challenger.

"Hmm, okay. If you say so," I replied as I got into his car.

"If you don't believe me, why get into my car? I ain't with no bullshit, ya hear me?" he stated, standing by the driver's side of the vehicle.

"Nah, we good; let's go," I said, leaning my seat back, getting comfortable on his leather seats.

As we drove back to campus, I felt nervous. He had been trying to get at me before now, so I wondered if he would be just like the rest. There was an empty parking spot right behind the building he could get. Heading to the door, I saw Royal calling me. Truth be told, I completely forgot about her. I answered quickly.

"Hey, girl, you all right?" I questioned while searching for my student ID to get us into the building.

"Bitch, where the fuck are you? You know we don't just leave without making sure the other one is good. Like, the fuck wrong with you?" she screamed into the phone, sounding drunk as a skunk.

"Look, I'm good. I ran into a classmate, and he brought me back to campus because I was tired, and he was coming this way." I smiled up at Eric as he held the door open for me.

Royal continued to go on a rant as we got on the elevator to take us to the third floor. Stopping the conversation to put my focus back on Eric, I politely disconnected the call, telling Royal I would see her when she got back.

I unlocked the door to room 315, with him following right behind me. My dorm was cute; it was a simple little two-bedroom suite. Royal had one side, and I had the other. The only thing I hated was that the walls were so thin that whenever she got her groove on, I could hear it late at night.

"So, you're safe and sound," he said, sitting on top of the table in the common area.

"Yeah, thanks to you." Sniggering at him, I said, "You wanna stay out there or come inside?" I slid off my skirt, revealing my purple satin panties.

He wasted no time. Undressing right in the living room area, he bent down, grabbed a condom from his pockets, and walked over to me. There was no foreplay, nothing sensual about the moment. Just straight fucking. He bent me over so I could touch my toes and rammed his cock deep inside me.

He let out a loud moan as I gasped. Gripping my waist tightly, he pounded my little tight pussy like he had a point to prove. The roughness of his stroke made my pussy wetter by the second. Keeping himself inside of me, we walked over to the table, where he told me to lie down.

He held my legs up as he slid back inside of me, then took my right foot, shoving it into his mouth. The way he moved his tongue around my toes to the way he flickered his tongue on my heels was such an experience. I enjoyed every moment of it. He pumped himself into me while my foot was still in his mouth. He would roll his back with every thrust, making me feel every inch. Then he grinded his dick in me in a circular motion, hard and fast. He was digging for my G-spot, and I know he found it that night.

Pulling out of me and flipping me on my stomach, he told me, "Arch that back, baby."

"Like this, babe?" I moaned back to him as I felt his fingers against my pearl.

"Yeah, just like fucking that," he snickered before shoving his dick into me. He held my waist, thrusting himself forcefully into me. My pussy loved how his dick felt as she throbbed and clinched on him. Moments later, as we were in the midst of the round, Royal came bursting through the door.

"Well, that's why yo' ass hung up on me," she said. "Well, don't mind us, Eric. Your little secret is safe with me. Come on, babe." Royal walked past us, leading the same guy I saw her dancing with at the party into her room.

That threw off the mood, and Eric was already halfway dressed before I could apologize for her actions.

"What's wrong? You don't have to go. Stay the night," I insisted, but his demeanor toward me changed.

He was uptight and distant. "Nah, I really need to go. I'll see you on Monday, OK?" Giving me a homeboy hug, he ran out of my room, and I didn't hear from him or see him until that Monday.

So, yeah, I felt entitled to see who that bitch was, and from all I knew, up until a few weeks ago, she was nobody to him. But Eric isn't leaving me like that, so whatever I have to do to get rid of her . . . I will.

Chapter 3

Eric

I was left alone with my thoughts and my rage. Man, I can't believe that bitch came over here. I noticed her calls, but I had no clue she would pop up. A ho needs to know a ho's place. I told her from the beginning that I just wanted to smash every now and then; plus, she knew I had a girl. I told her dumb ass I was done with her two weeks ago. She seemed cool with it. I thought nothing else about her. All this shit was a mistake I can't take back. I cannot believe this shit; I just lost it all.

I've never seen Reneece so repelled by me. When she shoved me, I knew she was hurt. Reneece didn't deserve this shit. She was so perfect. When I first met my girl, we were juniors in high school. I was new to the area, from DC, and being in Durham was like a culture shock. It was country and hood. I walked into my AP English class and saw her sitting there. She gave me the vibe of Keisha from *Belly*. Just a little lighter. Her smooth, brown skin, five-foot-six frame, thighs, and hips could make a man get down on his knees. I had to have her.

She ignored me and the little notes I left on her desk for a while, and I even went to the extreme of going through one of her favorite teachers to get her attention. It was Valentine's Day 2007, and the school was doing a fundraiser for prom. The candy grams were a hit, and that was my way in. Walking up to the fundraiser desk that morning, I purchased three single roses and the grams to be sent to her. One of the dance team girls asked me if I would add a note. So, keeping it simple, I wrote,

Hopefully, this will show you I was serious about making you mine. Not just for Valentine's Day but for all time. Here's my number. I'll be waiting for your call, my beautiful queen.

I thought I was so smooth, but looking back at it now, I probably sounded lame as fuck. Nevertheless, Reneece thought it was cute. After receiving my grams, she texted me and asked if we could meet after school. With every dude that sent her something, I was the only one she gave a chance to. She met me by the gym before basketball practice.

"Hey, Eric," she said, approaching me from behind.

Nervously, I responded, "Heyy, Reneece." Man, she looked amazing in her pink long-sleeved shirt with a bedazzled broken heart in the middle of her chest, and her red, Baby Phat jeans had her ass poking out something crazy.

"I thought your note was sweet. So, you really like me, huh?" she asked, coming closer to me. It felt like her eyes peered through my soul.

"Yeah, I like you, and I definitely want to get to know you and make you my girl if possible." I was subtly trying to shoot my shot. I leaned against the wall, feeling impotent to keep my eyes off her.

"Well, you can take me on a date after your game tomorrow night. I'll be there, being your biggest cheerleader." She kissed me on the cheek before departing. "I look forward to your call later and our date."

From that moment on, she was mine. Now, here we are, seniors in college, ready for the journey of life together—and I lost her. Nothing I was feeling could compare to the hurt I've brought her.

I should've avoided all of this months ago. I should've stopped after the first time. But sometimes, men can be weak, stupid, or just plain selfish. I met Dareen one night at a house party that my Kappa bros and I were having. We were celebrating the new line that crossed at UNC. Necce and I had been arguing, so at the last minute, she decided she would rather be with her girls than come with me. To be honest, we were having a rough time for months, especially with our schedules being so conflicting lately with work, school, clubs, and organizations that we barely had enough time for each other.

That same night, I met Dareen. I was fucked up off the Kappa juice. We were doing our stroll through the halls when I noticed her in that little skirt she wore. Her ass was all up in the air, no panties on, and she was flirting with every nigga in her path. When I came around her way, she was twerking and shit with one of her girls in the middle of the floor. She eyed me down, so I nodded for her to approach the corner where I stood. She was trying to tell me how she had been trying to get my number all semester, but I wasn't hearing anything she was saying. My dick was hard, I knew Reneece wasn't giving me any, and I was tired of having blue balls.

Some Drake song came on, and all I can remember is her soft phat ass grinding all over my dick. I had enough of the teasing by the time the song went off. Steering her toward a bathroom upstairs, I was going to get that nut off by any means. Her lips were so juicy I really wanted to see what her mouth could do. Pushing her on her knees, I unzipped my denim blue jeans, releasing this monster dick I got, and told her to open wide.

Her head game was weak. She was scrapping my dick with her teeth, making my dick soft. So, I pulled her up, moved to her back, and bent her over the sink. I may have been drunk, but I knew better than to raw dog shorty. I searched the cabinet by the mirror for a condom.

Locating a Lifestyle, I put it on. It was tight as shit around my dick, and it was too small for me, so I couldn't waste time.

I gave her hard, fast, deep strokes. Her pussy lips gripped my dick just right. I pounded her faster until the condom popped. She begged me to finish fucking her, but I couldn't take no chances like that. Pulling up my pants, I walked out of the bathroom, leaving her there.

After that night, she found me on Facebook. Everything on my social media surrounded me and Reneece. But she wasn't discouraged. I received a dm from her daily until I finally responded. That was my second mistake.

I would hit her up whenever me and bae weren't seeing eye to eye. About a month ago, I told her about Reneece and that I wanted to end things. She seemed okay before leaving her dorm. I never once led her on that we would be more than just occasional booty calls, so I wished her the best and planned on taking that secret to the grave with me.

I finally realized I couldn't keep it up. Cheating was the one thing I vowed never to do to any woman, especially after seeing how my dad treated my mom when I was younger and hearing her cry at night. I never wanted to be that guy. The more I fucked Dareen, the more I felt as if I was becoming more and more like him, so I ended it to save myself and my relationship.

As I mentioned, shorty seemed straight when I left. I never received any more inboxes, and I deleted her info from my phone and as a friend on the book. I didn't realize Dareen was going to act like this. After I didn't answer one of her calls last week, she started following me around campus. I thought nothing of it, but to show up unannounced at my home was a different story.

I planned on proposing to Reneece tonight. I couldn't have a life without her. There was no need to chase her. I needed to fix this and do whatever it took to get my wifey back. Finally getting up from the bottom stairs, I cleaned up all my things before going into the kitchen to pour a drink. I took a couple of shots of Patrón and looked at my phone. The only missed calls I had were from ole girl.

Since she wanted some drama, I was going to deliver it to her dorm room steps. Taking my bottle, I grabbed my car keys and headed out the door. I was halfway through town when she called me again, and this time, I answered.

"Hey, sexy daddy," she said, sounding all jolly before I could say hello.

"Yo, what the fuck, yo? You came to my house?" I screamed into my Bluetooth.

"I wanted to see you. Is that a crime?" she questioned with a laugh.

"You wanna see me? Word? Okay, yeah, where you at?" I waited for her to tell me where she was and pulled over to wait for her answer.

"You mad at me?" she queried.

"Nah, I'm good, man, but where you at?" I asked, probing her for the location so I could show out on her stupid ass.

"I have something really important to tell you," she pronounced. I could hear the wind blowing through the phone.

"Really? That would be what exactly? Is that the same reason you been following me like a stalker? I could lock you up for that shit if you don't stop," I said, telling her that I knew about her following me and I didn't want it to continue.

She sucked her teeth. "That wouldn't be a smart move. I'm late."

"Fuck you telling me for? I don't give a fuck what you late for," I uttered, deepening my tone.

"Bitch nigga, fuck you. I'm pregnant. I should've told ya little ugly-ass girlfriend that when I went over there, but

I thought you should tell her we're having a baby," she taunted me through the phone.

Raising my voice, I shouted, "Who the fuck you talkin' to? You better watch your tone with me, bitch." She simmered down some and got real quiet after I hollered at her.

"I'm at the football field. I was going to go out tonight, but if you're coming by, I won't." She gave me her location after a brief moment of silence. I let her know I wasn't far and would meet her on campus in a few.

Pregnant or not, she needed to learn not to fuck with people's relationships. She handled things the wrong way. Nothing in me believes she's pregnant, or at least, by me. I would catch a nigga coming out of her room while I waited for her to answer the door plenty of times.

So, I thought about it. I was going to make my move in silence but play her ass to the left and let my sisters have a conversation with her.

"You know what? You should go 'head. Go out. You must be going to Luna. That's all everyone keeps talkin' about," I said so I could set things up.

"Yeah, I was, but I'd rather be with you," she answered, trying to sound seductive.

Playing with her, I said, "I'll come by later tonight. Let me know when you get back to campus."

I wanted to find Neece, even though I knew she didn't want to see me. But I thought maybe seeing her and talking to her, we could work it out, and she would come home. Against my better judgment, I decided to call her twin sister, Davinece. I just wanted to see if she was with her. Before I could say hello, she spazzed out on me.

"Why the hell you callin' me looking for her?" she shrieked.

Taking a deep breath, I said, "Dee, I'm not in the mood for your shit. I'm just looking for her."

Sinisterly, she laughed out loud. "I'm not in the mood for your bullshit. You think she didn't tell me?"

"It's not your business. I don't know what she told you, but we're good. So, mind your own business and tell me where she is," I demanded.

Roaring back in the phone, she said, *"It's my sister, so it's* definitely *my business, nigga.* I knew she should have never fucked with your goofy-looking, Mekhi Phifer wannabe, ugly ass, li'l boy."

I was becoming infuriated with her sister. "I ain't tolerating no disrespect, shorty. If she wants to tell you, she can tell you. I gotta go."

Click.

Hanging up in her face, I searched my contacts, looking for anyone to help me find her. After scrolling back and forth for about ten minutes, I spotted the number of Jalisa, her best friend, so I called, hoping she would be helpful.

After a few rings, she answered in a whisper. "Hello?"

"Hey, Jalisa, I'm looking for Neece. Is she there, or have you talked to her?" I inquired.

She paused for a minute. She was moving around like she was trying to get away from whoever she was around. "Hey, E, ummm, yeah, she's safe. She doesn't want to talk to you right now. Honestily, I don't know when she will."

"Can you just tell her I love her? I love her so much, and I made a mistake and just want to talk. I want her to come home." I pleaded with her to give my message to Reneece, hoping she would be the reasoning voice behind our decision.

She groaned. "I'll tell her, but as your friend as well, you know you fucked up. I don't know if she'll ever forgive you, but maybe she will. But cheating, of all things? It's just wrong."

"Jay, listen, I know I did wrong. I know this whole thing is fucked up. Please have her come home or call me," I pleaded, hoping she would oblige.

"I will. Try to have a good night, bro." She exhaled before disconnecting the call.

"Thanks, Jay. I'll try," I replied, uncertain what would happen next. I put my iPhone 4S on the passenger seat before punching my steering wheel in frustration.

Eric's Prayer

I pulled over into the parking lot of the liquor store on Cornwallis, but before I went in, I had to pray. Not for me, but to save my relationship.

"Lord, I'm here to try to make things right. I need your help like I never have before. I messed up. Reneece is gone, and I feel like my whole world has stopped. She is the air I breathe and my reason for life itself. I need her in my life. No one knows how much I love her but you.

"I never wanted her to find out this way. Shit, if there were a way for me never to have told her, I probably wouldn't have. I need to figure out how to get my baby back. Tonight, I was going to commit to her completely. For all these years, Reneece has been my backbone. Now I feel like shit for deceiving her the way I did. I wonder if this is what it feels like when your heart is taken away from you.

"That bitch, Dareen, I got something for her. My sisters are going to teach her ass a lesson. I bet she won't show up at anyone's house again. Lord, I know it's not right for me to have those thoughts of Dareen, but she ruined my life and what I was accomplishing.

"Lord, please let Reneece forgive me. Lord, if I don't ask for anything else, please let me get my baby back. I need her. I learned from my mistake. I want to be all she needs because she is all I ever needed. I was just too blind and egoistic to see. Jesus, please, please, bring her back to me."

Chapter 4

Reneece

I watched Jalisa creep back into her bedroom. As I lay on her bed, and my tears stained her pillow, she asked me, "You okay?"

I sat up, looking at her while wiping my eyes. "Yeah, I just can't believe this." Again breaking down, tears streamed down my face. I felt like my whole soul had been ripped out. It seems like I loved Eric more than I loved myself.

She climbed on the bed beside me, wrapped her arms around me, and said, "Neece, it's your birthday. You are not going to sit and cry all fucking night."

"Yeah, some birthday," I stated gloomily, lying back down and pulling her green comforter over my head.

Yanking it from me, she insisted, "Neece, you can't be like that. You are stronger than this."

I shook my head and responded, "I just wanna be here."

Jalisa wouldn't stop bouncing on the bed. "No, you're going to get your ass up, take a shower, and get dressed. We are going out."

"Lisa, I don't wanna. Just let me be. *Fuck!*" I shouted at her.

She pulled the sheets until I fell on the bedroom floor, then sternly told me, "Bitch, I said get up. So, go 'head and get yourself together. We're going to go out. It's your birthday, and we going to turn the fuck up."

Jalisa left the room, leaving me on the floor to get myself together. I thought, *I can't let him have this much power over me. He's probably out fucking that bitch or some other ho right now.*

I was glad my bestie and I wore nearly the same size. I yelled to her that I was gonna take a shower and asked if she could find me an outfit to wear. Excited, she yelled yes and hurried me up to get myself together.

The water temp was scalding hot. I watched the mirrors fog from the steam before getting in. I hit shuffle on my iPhone, and "Milkshake" by Kelis came on.

With my washrag in hand, I used it as my microphone as I bellowed out the lyrics.

As the songs shifted gears to "Ring the Alarm" by Beyoncé, Jalisa peeked her head into the bathroom. "Neece, hon, you all right in there?"

"Yeah, girl, I'll be out in a few," I yelled back.

I could hear her laughing at me. "Okay, sis. I'll get us some drinks. I laid your clothes out on the bed."

I was stepping out of the tub when I could hear her heavy-ass feet walking by. Through the closed door, I asked where she was going, but instead of talking to me, she was mumbling to herself.

I came out of the bathroom to find Jalisa in the kitchen, phone on speaker, just ringing, while she mixed up some drinks. I was curious to know who she was calling, hoping it wasn't Eric. I stood in a corner to eavesdrop a little.

"Yo," a deep male voice answered.

"Hey, T, baby," she said, all giddy.

"What up, baby girl?" he responded, smacking all in the phone.

Taking a sip out of her cup, she replied, "Nothing. About to get in the shower. Just wanted to see what you were up to."

Smacking his lips, he said, "Word? Wish I was there to see that shit. You coming through? You know I got you."

I could see her smiling at the phone. "Hey, I may. It's my homegirl's birthday. Tryin'a see what she wanna do."

"Come through. I got y'all. Hey, babe, let me hit you back," he responded.

"Ok. Thanks, daddy," she said.

"You got it." He hurried off the phone, and I scurried back into the room, shutting the door behind me.

I sat on Jalisa's bed, staring at the outfit she laid out for me. She gave me two options. One was a mesh scoop neck dress, like nothing would be covered but my pussy, ass, and boobs. I may be at odds with Eric, but I wasn't going out nowhere like that. The second option was more my speed: a simple, all-red pencil skirt and a red and black bedazzled bustier.

I was applying baby oil to my legs when Eric's and my song, "Shawty" by Plies, played on my phone. *Maybe I should,* I thought while gawking at my phone. Picking up the phone, observing my locked screen of a picture of us when we won Mr. and Mrs. NCCU, I unlocked my phone and was about to call him when Jalisa walked into the room, snatching it out of my hand, exchanging it with a shot glass filled to the brim with Coconut 1800.

"No calls, no texts. Take a shot . . . or four," she said with a laugh, then smacked my ass. "Get dressed, girl. I'm about to shower."

After she got out of the shower, Jalisa turned on her party list, getting us crunk for the night. Before we left the house, we were feeling nice. We had about five shots plus her party juice. We took a few pics, posting them to the book with the caption, "When you nigga ain't actin' right on your birthday, you show out." I'm sure Eric was bound to see it, especially since he was tagged in it. I hope he realized what he was gonna be missing.

We headed to Club Luna for a party thrown by The Show Team. It was about 11:30 p.m., and it was packed with a line wrapped around the building. Good thing we knew everyone so we could just walk in. After finding a decent parking spot near the front of the club, Jalisa turned to me, telling me she was gonna see if her boo was already there.

Jalisa spotted her boo as she got out of the car to walk toward him. He was about six foot eight, built to perfection, and chocolate. He was something scrumptious. While I watched them from the car, I grabbed the blunt from the ashtray, took my first pull, and exhaled the smoke. Suddenly, I noticed that same ugly-ass girl, Dareen, walking in front of the car.

I hopped out of my ride without thinking twice and ran up to her from behind. I spoke no words before I grabbed the back of her nappy-ass weave ponytail. Then I quickly snatched her to the ground. Once she was on the ground, it was over. Kicking off my black pumps, I jumped on top of the beast, punching her repeatedly in the face.

Jalisa stopped her convo with Jay and ran to us, screaming, "Neece, Neece, Neece! Stop, girl, come on."

"Let me go! Bitch, let me go," I screamed, trying to break free from her grasp around my waist.

Security rushed toward us. I mentioned I was okay so that she would let me go. There weren't enough people to get me away from her nasty self. Sprinting at Dareen, I grabbed her ponytail again, this time snatching it out of her head, revealing her little rat-tail ponytail underneath.

"You bald-headed, bitch! That'll teach you to come to my house unannounced and uninvited again," I shouted, twirling the ponytail in the air.

"Your man invited me in plenty of times, if he even *is* your man," she taunted, lunging toward me.

She attempted to swing at me, but it looked like she had more enemies than friends. A short, light-skinned, chubby girl ran up to her from behind, jabbing her in the back. One of the security guards yelled for help as other girls approached, pushing me out of the way and jumping her.

"Come on, ho, let's go! Let's go," Jalisa screamed, pulling my arm. Once in the car, she slammed her door shut and scolded me. "What in the hell? Bitch, you are *Mrs. NCCU*. You can't be out here fighting and shit, and for what?"

Banging my fist on the dashboard, I said, "That's her! That's her! *She* ruined my life. The one who likes to come to people's homes."

Jalisa paused. "That's the girl Eric—"

"Yes. Okay? I took one look at her, wobbling in her heels, looking like a dust mop, and I lost it." I saw red. Had Eric been there, I would have fought him too. They both needed their asses handed to them.

When Jay arrived back at her home, Jay called Jalisa to make sure we were straight, and Jalisa told him we were good and that we had decided to go home. But in all actuality, she still planned on having us go out. While she talked to him, I gazed down at my hands, noticing my knuckles were red.

"You know we can't go anywhere like this. I'm going to call T and let him know that we're coming but will be a little late," Jalisa said, looking over my appearance.

"Yeah, I should probably wash my hands off and straighten up a bit, if that's okay," I said before I got out of the car.

"Yes, you most def need to get yourself together. I can look at you and tell you been in some shit. Come on, girl." Jalisa got out of the car, escorting me into the apartment.

Some people probably thought I was wrong, but I beg to differ. Someone had to teach that little ho a lesson. Since I couldn't finish it, I hope whoever those girls were completed the job for me.

Chapter 5

Dareen and Eric

"Where's my phone? I can't believe this shit," I screamed in annoyance. I just got jumped, and my homegirl didn't even help me.

"Dareen," Teericka responded softly, trying to get me to calm down.

Snapping my neck at her, I said, "No, you whack-ass bitches were no help. You let them jump me."

Teericka looked at my face real firmly. "Bitch, who the hell you talkin' to? I could've let all they asses jump you. Shit, you deserve every ass whooping you get."

"Tee, I don't know who you talkin' to. Don't you know who I am?" I inquired, tossing my ponytail on the car mat.

"A Greek groupie ho. The campus thot. A dumb ho who can walk back to campus 'cause I don't owe you shit." She shoved me out of her car, and I fell to the ground, watching her pull off as she threw my things out the window.

I stood around observing the people in the club line, all laughing and staring at me. I was getting angrier by the second. I didn't know who to call. After scrolling through my contact list two or three times, I decided to call Eric.

"Hello," I said.

"Yo," he responded dryly.

Huffing into the phone, making myself cry, I said, "Eric, can you come get me, please?"

"Where your girls at?" he asked, dodging my question.

"Look, we got into a fight, and she left me. Can you just come get me? That's the least you could do for your baby mother." I walked away from the club area down to the entrance of the parking lot.

He chuckled, like I just cracked a joke. "Well, you caught me at the wrong time. I'll hit you whenever I finish. Try a cab, shorty."

"What the fuck? Are you *serious?* Nigga, this is straight bullshit. If I was your bitch, you'd be coming to get me," I shouted into my receiver.

Catching an attitude with me, he said, "You right. And you're *not* my bitch. But if you don't stop disrespecting my girl, I won't be doing shit for yo' thot ass."

"Fuck you, Eric," I exclaimed.

"Yeah, well, if that never happened, I wouldn't be in the predicament I'm in now, right? I'ma get your ass a cab, or you can wait on the campus shuttle to come back." He hung up in my face without a chance for me to respond.

The campus shuttle pulled into the club parking lot to drop more students off. I was standing on the corner, hand on my hip, trying to figure out a plan. I never caught the campus shuttle, and every time I called Eric back, he ignored my calls. The shuttle was coming back down, slowly approaching me at the corner.

"Hey, hon, you not going in?" this buck-toothed, high-yellow-ass dude asked me.

"Nah, I forgot my ID or whatever. I was hoping my friend would come get me, but he ain't doing shit," I replied, rolling my eyes as my right leg twitched.

"Well, I don't mind taking you where you need to go. How far you stay from campus?" he solicited, smiling wide like the Kool-Aid man.

After hesitating, I jumped into the van, and told him I would ride with him to campus. I shot Eric a text saying:

Me: Got a ride, thanks for nothing.
Eric: Welcome.
Me: Still coming later?
Eric: Oh yeah, I'm still coming. I'll hit you.

Eric

I couldn't believe that ho asked me to pick her up. After what she did, she would be lucky to get a piece of twenty-five cent bubble gum from the corner store from me. I was at Club Passion, awaiting my sister Angie's arrival. My sister was a stud. She started dating girls in high school. No matter what, she was always ready for a fight. She's about five foot three, real chubby, keeps her hair in corn rows, and has our mother's caramel skin complexion. I was smoking my Jazz Wood Tip Black and Mild when she walked up beside me.

Giving me some dap, she greeted me. "Hey, bro."

"What's up, Ang?" I said, pulling her in for a hug.

"Everything all good. They took care of her ass. She'll think twice before doing pop-ups and shit." Taking my Black from my hand, she took a pull.

"Cool. Thanks, man. She hit me up talkin' 'bout she needed a ride. I think she's really stupid." I shook my head as I scrolled through Facebook and saw a picture of Reneece looking sexy as hell.

"Yeah, anytime, bro. You talked to Reneece yet?" she inquired while jumping on the trunk of my car to sit down.

"First, get your big ass off my trunk before you put a dent in it, but nah, she isn't talkin' to me," I told her, walking to the driver's side of my car to get another Black.

Jumping off my trunk, she said, "Give her some time. She called me and told me to meet her and Lisa at

Paradise. I'm going to head out there now. I'll let her know you love her and shit. Try to have a good night and be safe, bro."

I hugged my sister before we departed, going our own way. Then I sat in the car, wondering if I should try to call my boo. I reached into the glove compartment, moving my hand around until I felt the box I was looking for. The small black box I pulled out contained the engagement ring I went to pick up earlier this afternoon.

Part of me wanted to pull up at the club unexpectedly and propose. Then the other part was telling me to wait and give her time. It wasn't even twenty-four hours, and I wanted my baby. I missed her so much.

My phone began vibrating as it sat on top of my dashboard. Cranking up my car, my phone went off again. Instead of paying attention to the caller ID, I answered the call through my car's Bluetooth.

"Yeah, man?"

"You coming over still? I'm on campus." Dareen's voice was giddy.

I hesitated, not giving her a response, which made her attitude switch on.

She sucked her teeth. "Eric, are you still coming? We need to talk. . . . Hello . . . Damn, nigga, I know you hear me."

I took a deep breath and replied, "I don't wanna be bothered with you or anyone else."

"Your ho jumped on me, trying to beat my ass, then, out of nowhere, three fat bitches jumped me. Then I call you for help, and you give me your little ass to kiss. I had to ride that shuttle home. Nigga, I may be pregnant with your child, and this the fuck shit you do?" I yelled.

"I don't think I heard you right. What the hell did you just say?" I was trying to gain clarity.

"Eric, you fucking heard me. I'm fucking pregnant, like I told yo' sorry ass earlier. So you need to treat me with a little more respect," she sneered.

"And if you are?" I said, provoking her to see what she had up her sleeve.

"Nigga, is you serious? I could've said something to yo' little bitch, but I didn't. You just better be a good dad," she said, goading me.

Chortling at her, I said, "You fucked up my whole life. You know I strapped up with you every time, so you better go and play this game with someone else."

"You're an asshole," Dareen bellowed out into the phone, and I couldn't care less.

"Tell me what you thought I was?" I said, inquiring insolently.

"Eric, I'm sorry. Can you just come by so we can talk about this?" she beseeched me, softening her tone.

"I'll meet you in front of the Union. I'm not coming to your dorm. That's a little too much, don't you think?" Hopefully, she understood that I was conveying that I don't wanna be alone with her.

"Why?" she questioned, like I owed her any response.

I retorted back to her, "That's the deal. You wanna talk, meet me at the Union, or miss me."

"Fine. Let me know when you're close." I didn't even give her a response. I hung up the phone and made my way back to Durham.

Dareen

I couldn't believe this nigga. He would rather treat me like shit. I thought what we had was real. I need Eric to be the man I fell in love with. It was about midnight when he hung up on me. I wanted to show Eric everything he could have, so I gave myself time to shower quickly.

It was a little after midnight when Eric finally showed up. I was sitting in front of the Union on one of the park benches, smoking a blunt.

He approached me, uttering, "If you're pregnant, should you be smoking?"

"Hi, baby," I tittered.

"My name is Eric." He stood, his face wrinkled up in disgust, and his arms folded across his chest.

I couldn't stop cackling. I thought he was trying to be funny until I patted the empty part of the bench for him to sit next to me, but he wouldn't.

Declining gracefully, he said, "Nah, I'm good, yo. What the fuck were you thinking coming to me and my girl's crib? You that stupid?"

Calling out to him softly, I said, "Babe?"

"Stop fucking calling me that. You were wrong. I don't know if I can ever get her back." I took a deep breath after exhaling the smoke.

Hopping off the bench and coming closer to him, I said, "Eric, you don't need her. You have me. Let me be your everything. I love you," I pronounced.

Eric started guffawing uncontrollably. "You *love* me? Nah, ho, you don't love me. You love any man with a dick. Fuck out of my face, yo."

"Eric, are you fucking kidding me? I love you. I will do anything for you. Anything to be with you. And I'm telling you, if I can't be with you, no one else will," I declared, getting into his face.

"Are you threatening me?" he questioned, pushing me back.

"No, I'm *telling* you, baby or not, Reneece better watch her back if y'all do get back together. 'Cause *you will be mine,*" I asserted as he gripped my arms.

"Dareen," he said, "if you ever threaten or harm her, you will regret it."

"Why don't you care for me like you care for her? Don't you get it? I *really* love you. I would never leave you. What do you see in her that you don't see in me? When you were inside of me, you loved it. I know you did. I knew then, after that first night, this was meant to be," I said, trying to proclaim my love for him.

"No, I liked it, an easy nut. It's not because you were better in bed than her 'cause you're not. I fucked up, but I never told you I wanted you or wanted to be with you or that I was leaving my girl. I don't know what made you think that." Letting go of me, he walked toward the bench, standing beside it.

"But—" I started before he interjected.

"But *what?* I'll take you to the doctor in the morning to verify this pregnancy. You better never call or come near me or my girl again if you're not. You understand me?" he screamed at me.

"You don't mean that," I said forlornly.

"An easy ho like you fuckin' every new line of Greek niggas, I should've never fucked you. That was my fuckup. But tomorrow will determine how much longer I have to deal with your ass." He turned away from me and walked back toward the parking lot.

"Eric, you don't mean this. Look, a child is a blessing—*our* blessing. We can be a family and have it all. Come on now, are you really serious?" With tears filling my eyes, I grabbed his wrist, trying to stop him.

"Maybe I do, maybe I don't, or maybe I don't give a fuck 'bout you or shit you do. But know if anything ever happens to Reneece, and I find out you had anything to do with it, I will be coming for you." Then he yanked his wrist out of my grasp.

Eric walked to his car, and I watched him speed past me without any double take. Walking back down to my dorm, I whispered to myself, *I will have you, Eric. Reneece, watch out. Eric is mine.*

Chapter 6

Reneece

Two Months Later

"Reneece, you're going to be late," Jalisa bellowed.

"I'm coming, Lisa, gotdamn," I shouted from the bedroom as I examined myself in the mirror.

She ran up the stairs. "Neece, he's outside." She bent over, holding her knees like she was out of breath, before standing back up. Then she glanced over at me, "Yassss, bitch, you better mothafucking slay, bitch, yasss."

"I look good?" I asked, turning around one last time.

She snapped her fingers in the shape of an *S*. "You look damn good. Shit, I wanna fuck you in that dress. Go ahead and kill it. Make Eric sweat."

"Thanks, Lisa." I smiled at her after taking one last glance at myself.

She was right. I was one bad bitch. Eric and I had been working on fixing our relationship, and he's been making one hell of an effort. He wanted to take me out for a little date night. Since I was staying with my bestie the past few months, I think it made us reevaluate our relationship.

Eric ended up telling me about Dareen's fake pregnancy. It hurt, but at least he was honest with me. I appreciated his effort and honesty. Love is a crazy thing.

Some people might think I'm crazy for going back, but you can't throw it all away after one mistake when you're truly in love with someone.

When I got downstairs, he was standing there looking ravishing in his black, silk, button-down shirt that he had left open a little at the top, showing off the chain I got him for Christmas last year. His black slacks and pointed black dress shoes added a nice touch to his ensemble. With that fresh cut and lineup, his beard was growing too. Just looking at him made my pussy wet. After not fucking for almost three months, a bitch was ready to pounce on him like prey in the jungle.

Smiling at me, he said, "You look amazing. I don't even wanna go to dinner."

"You like it?" I asked, taking his hand into mine.

"Babe, you look amazing," he complimented, handing me the flowers he had placed on the table by the door before he escorted me outside.

Hand in hand, we walked down the steps when a black stretch Lincoln Navigator limo pulled up in front of the house. I was pleasantly surprised by the vehicle.

He opened the door and said, "Your chariot, my lady."

I stepped into the limo. "So, where we going?"

"It's a surprise." He slid in beside me, rubbing on my thigh.

As we approached our destination, Eric asked me to turn my head as he placed a black silk blindfold over my eyes.

"What are you doing? I wanna see," I said, gripping his hands playfully.

The limo stopped shortly after I was blindfolded. Directing me every step of the way as he held my hand, I could hear the sound of an elevator door opening and closing. Then we walked down a long corridor that felt like forever, and I was getting more anxious by the second.

"Okay, now, wait here," he said before kissing my lips.

"Eric, come on. You know I hate surprises, and this is enough. Babe," I called out.

Finally, he returned. "You ready?" he asked, helping me enter a room. I was shocked when he removed the blindfold.

Observing the beautiful scenery around us, I gripped his hand. "You did all of this for me? This is so amazing." It was, in fact, truly amazing. The room was lined with candles, and the scent of a birthday cake and a trajectory of red and pink flower petals directed us to the glass dinner table. I didn't know whether to be happy or nervous. Sometimes, if it's too good to be true, it's exactly that.

Eric led me to the table. "You know I would do anything to please you."

"A Thousand Years" was playing softly in the background. If nothing else happened tonight, those first few moments were enough. We sat awaiting the waitress or waiter to appear when I caught Eric gawking at me.

"You, you're so amazing, and I am so lucky," he said.

"Well, thank you. *This* is amazing," I replied, blushing.

Eric stood up, undressing in front of me. Then with a simple wink, he ran, doing a cannonball into the pool.

"Nigga, what the hell are you doing?" I asked, laughing at him.

"Come on, babe, get in. It feels great!" he said, swimming around.

"You can jump in naked all you want, but me—oh no." Standing on the pool's edge, I shook my head as I watched him enjoying himself.

"Babe, stop being all bougie," he taunted me, splashing around, getting water all over me before diving deep into the pool.

"Eric," I called out for him, but he wouldn't come back up. "Come up now, this isn't funny," I yelled.

Breathing heavily, he popped his head back up from under the water and set a black box on the edge of the pool. I ran to grab him a towel, and when I turned back, he was on one knee.

"Reneece Anna Moore, you are my everything. I don't know what I would do without you. I was way beyond blessed to have you take me back. I love you, I love you, I love you so much. You are the reason I wake up every morning wanting to be a better man than I was yesterday. You give me a reason to smile. And if I ever lost you, I would probably die. I cannot live the rest of my life without you and without you as my wife. Please, will you marry me?"

I dropped the towel on the floor in total disbelief and just stood there in that spot. "Did you . . . are you proposing . . . like *seriously* proposing to me?"

He drew closer to me, ring in hand, and said, "Yes. I want to know if you will be my wife." He opened the black box, revealing the square-cut diamond engagement ring.

"Yes. Yes, I will marry you, Eric—yes." Then I extended my hand to his so he could slide on my new rock.

We were embracing when his frat brothers, my sorority sisters, plus my bestie came from the main door to the pool area, congratulating us and ready to celebrate.

"What the hell are all of y'all doing here?" I said, surprised.

"You know we weren't going to miss this." Jalisa pulled both of us into her arms, hugging us tightly.

My line sisters, Ronda and Monica, were throwing up their diamonds in celebration while Eric's Kappa brothers ran in, congratulating him as well. His line brother Dezemick wanted to capture this moment, so he gathered everyone together while setting up his digital camera.

"I'm so happy for you," Monica said, hugging me before Dez could take the picture.

"Thank you. He means so much to me. Shit, if someone had said this is where we would be now, I wouldn't have believed it," I responded with happy tears filling my eyes.

Who would've have thought this was God's plan? At 23, who knew I would have earned two bachelor's *and* plan my wedding? Life couldn't get any more perfect than this.

Dear Diary,

Omg, I can't believe this. I'm supposed to be getting ready for our celebration party, but I just wanted to bring this to you. I need you to know that I am engaged. Who would have thought a few months ago that me and Eric would be here? Shit, I didn't. I was too busy crying my eyes out.

I'm glad I met him that night at the Greek Bowl. He loves me so much, and he's proving it more and more every day. He's taking his time to rebuild his trust with me.

He has truly put an amazing glow on me. I know I said that I was done, but things happen. That night we met at the Greek Bowl, he begged me for forgiveness, and I couldn't help but forgive him and try to move forward.

Since that night, I have never regretted any of my decisions. He has done everything right; sometimes, it feels too good to be true.

My mom is going to be so excited. Probably more excited about it than my ass, lol, considering how she was so ecstatic to know I was giving him a second chance.

I know one thing. Between all this excitement I'm feeling, plus this liquor, and the fact me and Eric haven't had sex in a while, shit, I'm ready to hop on that dick now.

I need him to take this pussy tonight, or I'm taking that dick. No questions asked. Shit, he better hope I don't take it at the club. If I get horny enough, I might. Especially since I ain't wearing no panties under the dress I'm 'bout to put on. Well, diary, that's my news for tonight. I'll tune in with you a little later.

Reneece

Chapter 7

Dareen

Andre was clutching my shoulders as I sucked on his balls. "Damn, bitch, you suckin' this dick just right."

Moving my mouth back to his dick and spitting on it before jacking it roughly, I said, "Yeah, you like it? Come on and climb in this pussy."

"Bend over, bitch," he instructed me, pulling me to my feet, bending me over the bed.

Andre was a tall, milk chocolate, rock-built dude. We met during a kickback at one of his frat brother's houses. It was immediate chemistry, and I wanted to get me a nut as much as he did. Learning from my mistake with Eric, I made sure I put none of my feelings into him.

I was giggling a little as I bent down, touching my toes. I looked back at him with a smirk, observing him jacking his dick while eyeing my naked body. As soon as he began sliding the head of his dick inside of me, someone banged on his room door.

Keeping his dick inside of me, he shouted, "Yo."

Another male's voice shouted through the door. "She said yes, brah. They're heading to Carmen's to celebrate. You comin'?"

"Word? Let me finish my workout and shower. I'll be ready in a few, or I can meet y'all there," he responded.

He penetrated my pussy gently, waiting on his friend to leave so he could finish fucking me. But I was curious and wanted to know what was going on.

"So, you gonna give me a quickie to go hang out with your friends?" I pestered, standing up and moving closer to the bed.

His hardened dick was in his hands while he approached me. "My homie Eric, him and his girl got engaged tonight. We gonna help them celebrate, but I ain't going nowhere 'til I bust open this pretty little pussy."

"What?" I shouted. I quickly gathered my T-shirt dress and bra and got dressed.

He stood there looking confused. "Where you going? Like, what the fuck is your problem?"

"I got to go," I said, tying my black Air Max.

Shaking his head, he pushed my legs open. "Bitch, you better get back here and let me bust this nut."

Closing my legs, I said, "Nigga, fuck you. I have something more important to handle."

I guess he didn't like being blown off with a hardened dick. Andre shoved me out of his room. "Don't come back 'less you going to let the rest of my niggas hit too, stupid bitch!"

Standing in the doorway with my middle finger up, I replied, "Fuck you, Andre."

"That's what you could be doing, but nah, you *gotta go,*" he said, slamming the door in my face.

I walked to the nearby bus stop, scrolling through my Facebook timeline to see if it was true. It's been almost three months since I saw Eric. I remember that last encounter as if it were yesterday.

He picked me up around seven in the morning. He got an appointment for me at the clinic downtown at the last minute.

He barely said two words to me during the ride there. It felt like the longest ride ever. I tried to grab his hand when we got to the clinic, but he moved away from me. We waited for about twenty minutes before a nurse called us to the back. After I pissed in the cup, the nurse took us to room four to await the doctor and the results.

"I'm so nervous. If we are pregnant, I hope it's a girl," I stated.

"Did you call the other niggas you fuckin' and tell them about your pregnancy? Shit, if you even are *pregnant." Eric rolled his eyes and refocused his attention on his phone.*

I lay down on the examining table, my arms folded, annoyed with his behavior. We just stayed there quietly until the doctor arrived thirty minutes later.

Knock, Knock.

"Dareen?" the doctor asked, popping her head in the door.

"Yes," I answered, sitting up.

Shaking Eric's hand, then mine, she introduced herself. "Well, I'm Dr. Grey. I understand you all came in to see if you are expecting your first little one."

I nodded my head as she went over my chart.

"Well, other than your blood pressure seeming a little too high, I can tell you that you aren't pregnant," she said, placing her clipboard on the table.

"Yes! Fuck yeah," Eric shouted in relief. "Hey, Doc, can I get that test result?"

"I mean, if it's necessary, I can have a copy made for both of you," she replied, confounded by his reaction.

"Please, so I can get back to campus." Eric stood up, shaking the doctor's hand. "You have made my day."

"Dareen, do you have any questions for me? I would like to set you up on some form on birth control," she said, sitting there in her Yachi wig and legs crossed with judgmental eyes.

"Nah, I'm good. I'll come a different day." I sat up and watched the doctor depart from the office. She instructed us to wait until the nurse returned with the extra test results before we left.

After receiving the documents, Eric scurried out of the office, leaving me in the dust. I caught up to him, and he was sitting in his car, taking a picture of the results.

"So, you couldn't wait for me?" I asked him, holding his driver's door.

"Bitch, if you don't move, I'm gonna pull off with you on this car. It's over, Dareen. We ain't got shit to talk about no more," he voiced, trying to push me out of the way.

"No, Eric, please. You know we can always try again," I proposed, but he laughed in my face, pushing me out of the way.

With his speakers blasting "Stay Schemin'" by Rick Ross, he backed out of his parking space. He chucked the deuces through his sunroof, leaving me to find my way back home without a second thought.

The sound of someone laying on their horn broke my thought process. One guy was waiting at the bus stop when I arrived, dancing to his own music. He looked up, nodded at me, then went back to dancing.

The first thing I thought of doing was calling Eric's phone. But when I did, an older lady answered the phone, saying I had the wrong number. I thought it was a game he was playing, so I called two more times. When the lady cussed me out for blowing up her phone, I knew then she wasn't hiding Eric from me.

I couldn't think of anyone who was friends with me and Reneece, or at least knew her so I could get the real tea. So, I went to my next best option: Facebook. I searched for both of their pages, under their line names, real names, even nicknames I've heard around the yard, but nothing came up. Then I realized that they both blocked me.

Thinking out loud, I said to myself, *If I go to Carmen's, I can see firsthand. Like, I know he was mad at me, but I mean, proposing to that ugly little bitch, Reneece? No. He is my happily ever after.*

After waiting about an hour, the bus finally came. The crisp spring air blew against my neck, giving me goose bumps. As I stepped on the bus, my phone rang. I slid my bus fare into the machine and walked to the back of the bus. It rang again before I could see my call log to call whoever it was back. Looking at my caller ID, I saw it was my girl, Joanna.

"Hey, girl," she exclaimed enthusiastically.

"Hey," I responded in a monotone, clicking on my home button to return to Facebook.

"You still out hoeing around?" she asked jokingly.

"Whatever. No, I'm headed to campus," I sneered.

"Well, let's go out. Don let me get the car, and I'm free tonight. It'll be fun. No drama," she insisted.

"Let's go to Carmen's," I suggested, hoping she would agree.

Enquiring about my club choice, she asked, "Why there? I was thinking 40/30. We can get in without being in line and paying."

Shaking my head, I said, "I heard something was going on there. I can pay for us if that's an issue."

"Hmm, all right. We can go, but if this is about some dick or you start some shit, you'll be left right there. I said *drama-free night*," she persisted, her tone hardening.

"Word? That's how you going to do me?" I asked, laughing at her comment.

"Yeah, bitch, 'cause you be on some bullshit sometimes, yo."

"Whatever," I said, sucking my teeth in the phone.

"Call me when you get to campus. I'll meet you in front of Eagle Landing."

After we hung up I continued to go through all my friends who might be near Reneece and Eric, but still no luck. It took me an hour to get back to campus. I waited in front of Eagle Landing, but Joanna wasn't there. So I went inside New Baynes to start getting ready. I was getting off the elevator when I ran into Jeff's sexy ass.

Jeff was one of Eric's line brothers. He was six-four, slim, had freckles over his high-yellow cheeks, almond-shaped eyes, and a swag to die for. All the girls threw themselves at him except for me. But if I really wanted to fuck him, I'm sure he would let me.

Purposely bumping into him, I said, "My bad, Jeff. I wasn't paying attention."

Turning around, facing me, he stated, "You good? What you got goin' on tonight? I'm going out to celebrate with one of my boys. It's gonna be turnt up, that's for sure."

"Aww, what y'all celebrating? You can't give a girl no invite?" I questioned, hoping he would give me some information about the engagement.

He just smiled at me. "A new beginning for two of my friends."

Cocking my head to the side, I said, "I'm supposed to be heading to Carmen's. I heard something was going on there tonight."

Leering at me, he said, "Word? I'm meeting everyone at Rumba. That's the plan for now."

"Really? I thought Carmen's was going to be jumping tonight. Maybe I should switch."

Abruptly, he insisted I stick with my plan. "No, I mean, you don't have to change. Like I said, it's a last-minute thing. We still figuring it out. I may slide through there if we aren't too turnt."

With a slight sigh and a smile, I said, "All right."

"Cool. I'll catch you later." Jeff walked off down the opposite hallway, leaving me pondering if he was telling me the truth or trying to keep me away.

I was turning by the elevator and heading toward my room when Joanna came off the elevator.

Running up beside me, she said, "What's up, girl?"

Giving her one of those church hugs, I said, "Nothing much. Look, I talked to Jeff, and I changed my mind. Let's go to Rumba instead. He said it's supposed to be poppin' tonight."

I could hear the aggravation in her tone. "A'ight. Well, we need to get dressed so we can go."

Joanna and I headed to Rumba around eleven thirty. I knew I was looking good. Once Eric saw me, he was bound to come to his senses. I decided to wear a short, bodycon purple dress with a keyhole cut out in the back.

We finally got to Rumba and stood in line for about fifteen minutes before getting in, and it seemed to be a decent little crowd. Once inside, the DJ was bumping some old-school hip-hop mix, keeping us grooving until the club got packed enough to play the real booty-shaking music.

Joanna and I walked over to the bar until the time was right to get up and mingle through the crowd.

It took a good hour or so, but the club finally got packed, and we hit the dance floor. Between the two of us, I know we drank a good $150 worth of alcohol. Joanna was dancing with some guy to "So Anxious" when the lights came on. He was trying to get her number when I looked around, noticing no sign of Eric or his bitch.

I left Joanna, wobbling my way to her car, heels in my hand, and feeling every drink hit me at once. I noticed a guy standing in the parking lot talking to someone. I could've sworn it was Eric.

Running up to the guy, I screamed, "You can't marry her! You're supposed to marry me."

"Bitch, get off my man," some tall, brown-skinned girl yelled as she quickly approached me. Before I could even protect myself, I was on the ground, and the tall girl was kicking me in the left side of my stomach. Joanna ran up, trying to help me.

The woman looked at Joanna. "Tell yo' homegirl to watch herself."

Joanna came to my defense. "Listen, I'm not sure what happened, but please stop. She's had a few. We both have."

"Aye, bitch," the girl said, kicking me one more time, "control your liquor and stay away from people's men." She and her boyfriend walked off, leaving me to Joanna.

The following morning, I woke up on Joanna's couch. The aroma of fresh coffee was in the air, and Joanna was sitting on the floor watching *A Different World*. When she turned around and saw that I was awake, she went into the kitchen and poured more coffee, this time for both of us.

"Hey, thanks," I said, taking the steaming coffee cup out of her hands.

"Yeah," she scoffed, barely wanting to look at me.

Getting off the sofa, I walked over to her TV. "What's with the attitude?"

"You are fucking crazy, yo. I told you no drama." She was irritated, and it was all in her body language.

"What are you talkin' about? Didn't you have fun last night?" I asked, placing my cup on top of her entertainment center.

Looking at me, she asked, "What do you remember from last night?"

"Not much, really," I replied honestly.

Joanna stood before me and said, "Well, you attacked some dude, thinking he was Eric. Then his girl jumped on you. I had to get her to stop. You still on that nigga?"

"Joanna," I muttered.

"Nah, this is bullshit. He was never your dude, and you knew that. And in all honesty, you *are* a ho. There's not a nigga in the fraternity or on a basketball team you haven't slept with," she said aggressively. I had nothing to say, so Joanna continued her rant. "You know he didn't and never did want to be with you. That shit isn't cute. You need to get yo' shit together."

"Fuck you. What kind of friend are you? I love him, and we *will* be together," I hollered.

"Dareen, you're delusional." Joanna unlocked her phone, showing me a picture on Facebook of them. "Look, they're engaged; they're happy. Leave them alone. Stop being a dumb-ass thot, stop fuckin' everything with a dick, get your degree, and get right."

"He doesn't need or love her," I said, smacking her phone out of her hand.

"You're a dumb-ass ho. You need therapy or some shit. When you're ready, I'll take you back to campus." Joanna attempted to brush past me, but I grabbed her.

Clasping her arm, I said, "Man, fuck you. You don't understand what we have."

Laughing out loud at me, she replied, "You probably would if I let you. If you understood what kind of friend I am to you, you wouldn't be so upset. Now, let me go."

I released her arm, pushing her into her dining room chair. "Whatever. I don't need you to take me home. I think I have money for the bus."

"Hopefully, one day, you'll see and understand. I'm always your friend, but I'ma always keep it real with you," Joanna stated, returning to the kitchen.

"Yeah, whatever," I said, not hearing the bullshit she was tryin'a say.

Something came over me. I was looking for my shoes, and all I could think about was the picture Joanna showed me, everything she said, and seeing Eric and Reneece looking all happy and in love. It was supposed to be me.

I picked up my purse from the sofa when I noticed this beautiful glass vase she had sitting on a nightstand. I placed my bag over my right shoulder, my heels under my right arm, and then picked up the blue crystal vase. Joanna's back was turned, mixing up what looked like pancake mix near the sink. Quietly as possible, I approached her from behind. I gently put my heels on the tiled floor, hoping not to make her aware of my presence.

With both hands free, I swung the vase at her head. "*You're* the stupid bitch. If you're friends with Reneece, tell her I'll be coming for her next." Then I grabbed my shoes and ran out her back door.

Chapter 8

Eric

Two weeks later, I still floated on cloud nine after Reneece agreed to marry me. Life was getting better, and I was happy to have my baby back completely to myself. I was lying in bed when she entered our bedroom in a long trench coat and heels.

"You still watching this?" she asked seductively.

"Mmm, maybe," I said with a sly grin. Reneece unplugged the TV, so I couldn't just grab the remote and turn it on again. I assumed she wanted no distractions.

She then played "Rocket" by Beyoncé on the iHome stereo. As she danced in front of me, my manhood began to rise. Lewdly unbuttoning the trench coat, she then dropped it down to the floor, revealing her naked body. I unbuttoned my jeans, slipping my hand into my boxers, slowly caressing my dick. The way she moved her body so erotically made my body temp heat up.

She crawled on the bed, first pulling my pants off me, then slowly making her way to my dick. Straddling me, the wetness from her pussy seeped through my cotton boxers. She grinded her body on my groin slowly, matching the beat. My other head had thoughts and took complete control of the situation.

"You know when I say I do, you're stuck with me forever?" She leaned over, placing a kiss on my lips.

"I wouldn't have it any other way. Come here, beautiful." Pulling her back to my lips, I gave her tongue kisses, biting her lip, then taking my left hand and pulling on her hair. When she tossed her head to the side, I sucked on her neck as if I were a vampire trying to suck all her blood from her.

Reneece was breathing heavily, her temperature rising with mine, and her pussy getting wetter by the second. I seized her neck in my right hand as if to choke her. She tossed her head back and let out soft moans as I kissed my way down to her perky DD-cup breasts. Then I nibbled on her nipples, sucking and teasing them gently.

"You want daddy's dick?" I whispered in between sucking on her nipples.

"Yes, daddy. Fuck me. Give me my dick," she pleaded, and I planned on giving her exactly what she desired.

Pushing her body back onto the bed, I removed my boxers, letting my horse free to do as he pleased. My baby wasted no time opening her mouth wide, allowing me to enter her cavernous mouth slowly. She held my thighs as I fucked her face. I T-bagged her, hitting her tonsils until she gagged.

Then I removed my dick from her mouth, kissed her lips, and moved my way down to her bald, phat pussy. Before entering her, I wanted a taste. Spreading her legs and putting them on my shoulders, I began to devour her pussy.

I slowly let three of my fingers enter her pussy as I sucked on her pearl. Reneece grabbed my head, grinding her pussy on my face. Her juices covered my face. I relished those juices as I stimulated her pussy with my fingers.

Lifting my head, I leaned back and removed my fingers so I could ease inside of her tight wetness. "You ready?" I asked her, tapping the head of my dick on her swollen clit.

Nodding, she grabbed my dick and helped me inside of her. I moaned softly as she moaned with the simple stroke. I was pumping into her tightness as she gripped my dick with every stroke. We were just getting started when Jalisa came yelling at us.

"You gave her a key?" I asked, trying not to lose focus.

"That's not important right now. Just keep going, baby." She placed her hands on my face, and we stared into each other's eyes.

"She'll have to wait," I stated, breathing heavily and pulling my dick out. Then I flipped her body over.

Reneece arched her back perfectly. Her round, chocolate ass tooted in the air, her arms dangling on the edge of the bed. I couldn't help but admire all that booty in front of me.

I took a handful of her hair as I pushed deeply inside her. I showed her pussy no mercy. While her ass bounced on my dick, I spanked her with one hand as I still held her hair in the other.

"You gonna take this dick, bitch. You hear me?" I moaned out, giving her every inch of me.

Her ass clapping back, her pussy talking to me, Reneece moaned louder and louder. "Take this fuckin' pussy. Mmm, fuck, yes. Take this motherfuckin' pussy."

I loved when she talked that shit to me. I fucked her harder. Stroking her deeper, I let go of her hair, used both of my hands to grab her waist and sped up my stroke. She was going to come on my dick before we went or did anything else.

Pulling out my dick, I told her to ride me. She crawled over to me, taking my dick into her mouth. She spit on my dick, then jacked it roughly. She continued jacking it as she placed both of my balls in her mouth. As she juggled them back and forth, she did this thing with her tongue, almost tickling my sack.

"Damn, babe," I said to her, looking at her when she released my balls and put my dick back into her mouth.

My dick wasn't wet enough before her friend came again, banging on the bedroom door.

"Are y'all done yet? There's someone here you need to see! It's important," she yelled through the door.

"Man, is it life or death? 'Cause we busy, Jalisa. Damn," I shouted, wanting her to go away.

"Man, it will be more than that if we keep bullshitting," she said. I could hear her stomp away.

Reneece took my dick out of her mouth. "Let's just see what she wants. Then we can get back to us."

"Yeah, and I'm taking that key back," I said, pissed that I had to walk around with a hard dick when I was in the middle of getting my first nut.

Reneece came over to me. "Don't worry, daddy. I'm gonna take good care of you when she's gone."

With a simple peck on my cheek, she got up to go into my dresser to find something to throw on for the time being. She tossed me a T-shirt and basketball shorts. "Hopefully, your print won't show in these." she joked.

"Yeah, well, hopefully, we can get her out of here ASAP, so this dick can get back in my pussy." I walked up behind her, pressing my still-hardened cock up against her ass and placing one hand in between her thighs.

"Well, if you keep teasing me, she won't leave, and we won't make it out of this room. Come on." Reneece tapped my hand like I was a naughty child.

I followed her after she threw on my Ninja Turtles T-shirt and some panties. Jalisa and some other light-skinned chick were sitting in my living room, talking.

"Seriously, Jalisa, we were busy. So, this better be good, and who the hell is this?" Reneece asked, standing beside me.

The two of them looked up at Reneece and me. "Well, I'm glad you put that on pause. We need y'all out here," Jalisa said.

Taking my fiancée by the hand, we walked farther into the living room. Before we could get any answers, my doorbell rang. We looked at each other. Then I left Reneece standing in the middle of the floor as I went to the door. I looked through the peephole, and there was Jeff and Reneece's line sister, Dana. I let them in, greeting them as they came into the house.

Growing curious about why our closest friends and this stranger were in my home, it was time to start asking questions.

"So, is anyone else coming, or can I know who this is sitting on my couch, not saying two words, with her eyes covered in the shades?" I asked, taking Reneece by the hand and going to sit on my gray suede love seat on the opposite side of the room.

Everyone sat silently, like they were afraid to speak. "Well . . . Is anyone gonna say anything? Or do I have to kick y'all out 'til you get balls to say what you need to?" Reneece asked, agitated.

"Fine. This is Joanna. She's friends with that girl, Dareen. Remember her?" Jalisa questioned, looking directly at me.

"Yeah, man. I haven't seen or talked to that stupid-ass ho in months. I left her ass at the clinic once I got the results showing she wasn't pregnant. Reneece knows all that," I said, holding my girl's hand.

"Yeah, that's true. That's why Eric transferred to NC State to give us a clean slate. So, what's the issue? Why is she coming up now?" Reneece probed.

"Man, that girl came to my room, tryin'a let me hit. She said to me she would give me some pussy if I told her where you guys were," Jeff chimed in.

"So, you gave her me and my future wife's information for some pussy?" I got up to lunge toward him.

"Man, you *know* me." Jeff moved out of the way before I could get to him. "I would never give anyone—especially her—anything about the two of you."

Sitting down again beside Reneece, her line sister, Dana, moved closer to the mysterious girl wearing the shades. Reneece watched the two whisper.

"The fuck y'all whispering about? You're in *my* fuckin' home, so either speak so we can all hear you or get the fuck out," Reneece yelled at them.

"Listen, what we have to say it's a bit concerning. I just wanna make sure once we tell you both that we handle this with the police. No other way," Dana stated, turning her head and looking out the window.

The mysterious girl finally removed her shades, revealing a swollen eye and bruises over her face. She looked around the room. "My name is Joanna. I used to be friends with Dareen. I came to Dana for help because she is one of my friends as well, and I knew she would make sure you knew what was coming."

"What the hell are you talking about?" I asked, leaning forward. "Gotdamn it, y'all keep talkin' in circles and not saying shit."

Joanna spoke again. "Dareen is upset that even after not seeing or talking to you all this time, she still doesn't believe you two belong together. She believes she and Eric do."

Joanna had an envelope in her hand. I snatched it, seeing it was addressed to Reneece. "Is this from her? Why is she sending my fiancée a letter?"

Reneece looked over my shoulder, seeing that it was indeed made out to her.

"Yeah, Eric, why is she writing me? Have you been fucking her again?"

"I don't fucking know why she's doing this. I've done everything in my power to keep away from that crazy ho. I've been nothing but honest. You have to believe me," I pleaded, throwing the letter on the table.

Joanna looked up. Her black eye was dark, and she looked distraught. She said, "I can answer that as well."

Reneece turned her head and faced Joanna. "Well, spit it out. 'Cause right now, none of this is making any fucking sense."

"Dana said I should be the one to talk to you about this, but after we read the letter and what she did to me, just in case, I had everyone come . . ." Joanna started her spiel but couldn't finish.

Reneece interjected. "Okay, *and?* Like, bitch, what the fuck are you doing here? Are you tryin'a set us up? You better start fucking talkin' before you have another black eye—or worse. You taking way too long to explain nothin'."

Reneece lunged at Joanna, but Jalisa grabbed her. "Reneece, just listen to her. Shit!"

Joanna moved out of Reneece's way, closer to Dana. "I have no problems with either of you. But Dareen, she does. She's crazy. She's obsessed with Eric. When she heard from some dude on campus she was fucking that y'all got engaged, she wanted to go where y'all were celebrating. When she figured out me and Jeff knew, she threatened our lives. She believes she and Eric need to, and should be, together. She wants him, and she won't stop 'til she has him."

Reneece looked at the note, not reading it at all, then back at me and asked, "I'm gonna ask your ass again. Have you seen her?"

Pulling her in front of me and looking deeply into each other's eyes, I assured her, "No, I haven't. I never will."

"I don't know you, and I don't know what's in the letter. But I do know she's been trying to find Eric for the past few months but couldn't, so as her friend, I tried to get her to let it go, let all of this go. Get her to understand, but she doesn't. Something's mentally wrong with her." Joanna hung her head.

Reneece looked at Joanna, shaking her head. Then she read the note out loud.

Hey, Bitch. I wish I could be happy for you, but I'm not. You stole my man. I love him. I thought you would've left him so we could be together, but you didn't. So just know I will fuck you up and, if necessary, kill you to have Eric. He's mine.

After she read the note out loud, I was filled with rage. I was ready to hurt someone. I told Joanna, "Tell that ho she doesn't have to look for me. I'm coming for her," and walked away. Reneece waited for Joanna to say something, but she never did. Reneece said, "Tell her, 'No worries, bitch. I got her,'" and walked off.

Chapter 9

Reneece & Dareen

Eric was still standing outside after everyone had left. I walked out on the balcony, where he was facing the trees, rolling up another blunt.

"Everyone gone?" he asked, looking back at me.

"Yeah, babe," I responded, walking up beside him.

"I don't want you to worry about anything. I'm gonna take care of this," he muttered.

"What you mean? What are you thinking?" I probed, trying to get inside his head.

Without saying a word, he pinched my cheeks before walking back inside the house. Following behind him, I closed and locked our patio door. I could hear music blasting from the bedroom. Lil Boosie's "Set It Off" was in the background, and as Eric puffed, he was rapping along.

"You wanna talk shit? You wanna run ya mouth? You want some gangstas front yo motherfuckin' house? We'll set this bitch off—"

Interrupting his rapping, I said, "Babe?"

"Yo," he responded, exhaling the smoke and holding the blunt out to me.

"You all right?" Removing the blunt from his hands, I sat at the foot of the bed and took a hit.

Rising, I said, "No, I ain't. Man, this bitch has lost her mind."

Passing the blunt back, I told him, "You know I'm good, babe. She just blowing smoke."

"Reneece, this ho is crazy, and I be damned if she, or anyone else, threatens or harms you. So, she wants to see me. Well, I'm going to make that happen, but I'll be the last nigga she sees." Putting out the blunt, he went over to the closet.

"Where do you think you're going?" I questioned.

"I know where she hangs out. I'm gonna find her, like I said. I told her months ago 'bout saying slick shit like that. Now, she wanna pass notes like we in high school or some shit. Nah, fuck that." He was incensed, and I knew there was no calming him down once he got this way.

"Eric, fine, you do that. Then what? Go to jail? We gotta be smarter than this. Maybe we should go to the police first, cover our asses, just in case something goes left," I advised.

Throwing up his middle finger, he exclaimed, "Man, fuck 12."

"Eric, I think the best way to do this is to take everyone with us *and* the note. If they don't handle it, then we handle it our way. They have no choice but to take us seriously," I said.

He hung his head, sighing deeply. "Reneece, it's not going to help. I haven't seen the police take care of us yet. You think they gonna take this note seriously?"

"Eric, she *threatened* me. We have witnesses who can vouch for everything this girl is possibly plotting to do to me. Let's try it my way, and if something happens later, it'll be self-defense," I said.

After a little more discussion, Eric finally submitted to my request. I called Dana and Jalisa, telling them to grab Joanna and we would go to the police station. As I made my calls, so did he. Calling Jeff was his first option, and he was all the way down. Then he called his sisters, telling them about the note and our current plans. His sisters agreed to be my "bodyguards," in a sense. Once everyone was in position, we gathered our things and made our way to the Durham Police Department.

Dareen

I was feeling really good today. I had just come from the seafood place down the street from campus and decided to sit at the Union to eat lunch. Campus was thinning out. Many people were preparing for graduation, some preparing to leave for summer break, but I was stuck here since I was behind in my grades. There was no academic probation, but I needed summer school and a whole extra year before I could walk across the stage.

I was walking through the Union, noticing the seniors picking up their caps and gowns, and I accidentally bumped into the girl in front of me.

"Oh, I'm sorry," I said, apologizing.

"You good." The young lady turned around, and it was Joanna. Her eyes widened like I was a ghost when she saw it was me.

"Joanna, what's the problem?" I asked, pushing up on her.

Gritting her teeth together, she said, "Dareen, you're crazy. You damn near tried to kill me! I'm one of the only true friends you had, and you tried to kill me for telling you the real. So, get the fuck away from me."

Clutching her by the wrist, I pulled her toward the women's bathroom. I looked at her with a crazed look in my eyes. "Did you give that ho my note?"

"Get your hands off me. Dareen, I loved you like a sister, but you need to let all this shit go. Find you a good man, one who will love you and *wants* to be with you, and vice versa. Leave them alone." Joanna jerked away from me.

My voice grew louder, as I yelled, "He *will* want me! That bitch is just in the way, but not for long. You'll see. Everyone will see. It's gonna work out. And you are going to be my maid of honor."

She put her finger over her lips to hush me like a child. "As someone who wants to still give a shit about you even after what you've done to me, you need just to walk away. Walk away from it all."

Joanna looked at me as if she really cared about me, but I felt it was all a front. I moved out of her way, allowing her to leave my space. I watched her scuttle out of the Union without ever looking back.

I left the Union myself, heading toward the back patio area. Before I could sit down, one of the campus police officers approached me.

"Hey, Miss Lady," he said, advancing toward me.

"Hey, Officer Brandon, how are you?" I smiled at him. He was the epitome of white chocolate. Officer Brandon had the prettiest blue eyes and tattoos over his neck and arms, and he was packing. Yeah, I fucked him, not once, but a few times. It was great too.

He gawked at my body. "I'm doing very, very well."

"That's great," I brushed over his arm seductively.

Pushing me away softly with a chuckle, he said, "Yeah." Then he paused slightly before saying, "Dareen, I need you to go with me to the campus security building."

Licking my lips, I asked, "Isn't it too early? And I thought you felt guilty, or did you leave your wife?"

His smile turned cold. "Nah, it's not that type of party. You're in some serious shit. So, we need to head there now."

"What you mean?" I questioned before going anywhere with him.

"You can either come with me, or the Durham PD will come get you. Your choice." He stood there waiting for me to decide.

I looked at Brandon and could tell he wasn't joking around. I agreed to go, just to know what was going on. Little did I know, shit was about to get real.

Dear Diary,

I can't believe this. We have been so happy for these past few months. I'm engaged to the man I love, and then here comes his thot-ass side ho.

How does this shit happen? She's still stuck on his dick? She can't tell he don't want her? Didn't want her? I know one thing, she got me fucked up if she thinks I will back down if she comes for me.

She is coming for me, sending threats and shit. Bitch, I will kill her. I can't wait to see this gorilla ape-looking-ass bitch again. She thought that night at the club she got fucked up was bad. This time, the damage is going to be worse.

If I find out Eric still fuckin' her or any bitch, especially after I gave him another chance, ooohhh, he's dead. He will never get this back. Him and his ring can go to hell.

As much as I want Eric to handle this shit his own way, we about to graduate college, start our careers, and no one has time for this bullshit. So, yeah, we went to the police. Trying to do things the right way, you know?

Dareen is not safe. They going to be worried about us, but they should worry about her. I got that ass. I never been so livid. I want that ass on a plate. When I get her, she's going to know what a real bitch like me will do to her when threatened. Don't play me. I may be sweet, but I ain't no punk-ass ho either. She better watch out.

I'm going to need a drink and a release for this aggression right now. So, diary, I'll be back. Let me go find zaddy and get some of that dick. Maybe that will help both of us right about now.

Reneece

Chapter 10

Eric

The past twenty-four hours have been hell. We were sitting at home watching *Paid in Full*. Reneece was cuddled up under me, and we were having a mellow moment to ourselves when I received a call from the police department.

"Hello?" I answered, clearing my throat.

"Hello, may I speak to Eric Walsh, please?" the male on the other end asked.

"Yes, this is he." I tapped Reneece on the thigh, motioning for her to get up as I placed the phone on speaker.

"I'm Detective Peterson. I wanted to get statements from all the parties that know anything about this situation and, if necessary, get you and your fiancée a protective order." I could hear him rustling papers around.

"Sure, let me see if we can get in touch with everyone, and we'll come down." I looked at Reneece, and with a simple nod, she got up from the couch and grabbed her phone to make the calls.

"Great. When you get to the station, tell them you are here to see Detective Peterson, and they'll handle the rest." He was sucking his teeth as if a piece of meat was stuck between some.

Around thirty minutes later, Jeff, Joanna, and Jalisa arrived at our home. Everyone dressed in black like we were about to commit a crime or attend a funeral. We rode down to the station in Reneece's 2012 Ford Explorer. The ride wasn't filled with conversations. It was more silent than anything.

When we got closer, Joanna asked us, "Why did they want all of us? Do you think they got her already?"

"Hopefully. If not, they better before I gut her ass," Reneece whispered as she searched for parking.

We went in as a united front, ready to move forward with our lives. We waited in the lobby area until Detective Peterson came out of his office. Reneece ran into one of her classmates and was up talking to one of them when Jeff tapped my arm, pointing down the hall, where Dareen was coming down.

I couldn't get up fast enough before Dareen took off, yanking on Reneece's golden brown tracks and pulling her to the floor. Reneece shrieked as she hit her head on the tile floor.

"Bitch!" Dareen yelled as she swung at Reneece, but before the punch could land, the police grabbed her.

Another officer and I helped Reneece off of the ground. "You all right, babe?" I asked, caressing her cheeks. "Y'all going to arrest that girl for assaulting her?" Redirecting my energy, I turned toward the police holding Dareen.

Dareen was observing Reneece and me. "When I get out of here, I'm going to kill you. Y'all hear me? It's the only way he'll be with me, I *know* it. And you know *he's mine*. It won't be long, Eric, baby. I'll see you soon."

"Bitch, he don't want you. Go get the help you need, sick ass. Maybe I should send you wedding pictures. That way, you can see the truth—or maybe kill yourself," Reneece shouted back as I held her waist.

Dareen was taken in the back by three officers, and finally, Detective Peterson came out of his office, looking around at the commotion and seeming confused. A lady officer approached him, whispering and pointing at all of us. After his sidebar with her, he came over to us.

"Eric and Reneece, I'm sorry this happened. Reneece, I understand you want to file charges for the assault?" He waved at us to follow him to his office.

We walked down a short hallway to his small office. It was simple: two brown chairs, a desk with a few pictures of his family, and a plaque honoring him for fifteen years of service on the left side of the wall.

"Sit down, you guys," he signaled at the chairs.

Without hesitation, I asked him, "Detective, how safe are we if, and when, she's released? You saw the tail end of everything, but the other officers saw everything, and we can tell you how crazy she's acting, even here, as if this isn't a police station. Who's to say when she gets out and comes for us, then what?"

"Eric, you do what you must to protect yourself and your family. But don't go looking for trouble. If she's released, don't look for her. Let her put herself in a fucked-up situation. Excuse my French," he muffled. "If she's released, just don't go looking for trouble. If she still wants to do something, let her trespass, then you react. Same thing for you, Reneece. You don't make a move on her unless she's done something to you. I'm telling you, until that comes into play, enjoy life. Don't let this stop you. You all keep living. Hopefully, she'll move on with her life."

"Okay, and if we make sure we call you all first and don't provoke her, then what, huh? She shouldn't be able to get away with all her shit," I exclaimed.

"Eric, please, calm down. I understand you and your fiancée's concerns and frustrations. But we have to let the law run its course. Just keep yourselves protected, okay?" Sliding the restraining order over to us, he stood and opened the door.

After I shook his hand, we gathered our crew to go home. After everyone got out, I told Reneece to wait in the car as I drove. I had a surprise for her. I figured we both needed something to make us smile.

"Well, no blindfolds," she insisted. "I think I can handle whatever you're about to throw my way."

I drove down the expressway with one hand on the steering wheel, going 70 mph. Jagged Edge's "Let's Get Married" played on the radio, and it had me thinking.

Glancing at her, I said, "Tomorrow, let's go downtown and get married. We can plan your dream wedding later or after graduation. But right now, all I want to do is to get married to you. You are my dream. Everything else can fall into place later."

Reneece grabbed my hand. "Womb to the tomb."

"'Til the casket drops," I responded.

Exiting off the highway, I pulled into a quiet little neighborhood filled with new houses and townhomes.

Pulling out a simple red box, I said to her, "Well, I was going to wait until graduation, but I figured, why wait?"

She took the box out of my hand. "What's this?"

I just smiled. "Open it and stop with the questions."

Raising one eyebrow, she said, "Nah, nigga, tell me."

Taking a quick glance at her, I insisted, "Just open it, big head."

Reneece opened the box, and as she tried to speak, she started to choke on her own spit. Finally, she cleared her throat. "Are these . . . It's keys. . . . House keys?"

Pulling up to our new home, I said, "Yeah, babe. Why don't you try them out?"

Putting the car in park, I unlocked the passenger door. Reneece jumped out of the car. "You seriously went and bought a house?"

I exited the car behind her and said, "Yeah, just closed on it. I was going to wait 'til you said, 'I do' before I gave you the keys. . . . In case you changed your mind."

She laughed and said, "I'm saying I do, regardless. I'm going to be so proud to be your wife."

Picking her up, I replied, "No, I'm going to be truly honored to be your husband."

I gestured for her to unlock the door to our new home. We walked into the three-story townhome, and her eyes bulged as she looked over the space. The sun was starting to set as we toured the home. We made it up the first set of stairs, where there were two bedrooms, a bathroom, and a den. We looked to the right and saw the den with a balcony.

"Baby, I don't need to see anything else. This is so perfect." Reneece opened the doors to the balcony, taking in the peaceful scenery surrounding us.

"See how tranquil this is? I thought this would be the perfect place to start our new lives, Future Mrs. Walsh." I placed my hands around her waist and rested my chin on her right shoulder, but just having her in my arms made me horny.

We moved back into the den. Unable to keep the sexual tension down, I unbuttoned her jeans, sliding my hand down her pants, and moved her panties to the side so I could finger her as we made out. Reneece pushed me away from her, biting on her lip.

"What you want, baby?" I slowly removed my shirt, revealing my decently built body. And my body was just right for her. She walked over slowly and seductively and pulled down my black Levi's and boxers. I returned the favor, slowly unhooking her bra and gently sliding her shirt above her head. Then I removed her jeans and purple silk panties. I was ready to take her.

Pushing Reneece against the wall, I nibbled on her neck, forcing my hands in between her thighs, and began to play with her pearl. Reneece could barely control herself as I rubbed it.

Her legs began to quiver as she wrapped her arms around my neck. She dug her nails deep into my skin and began to moan louder and louder. I felt her juices all over my hand and realized she was coming, so I stopped.

She sucked all the juices off my fingers while unbuckling my pants, releasing my manhood. She then slid down to her knees, caressing my balls with one hand and stroking my dick with the other.

Reneece had me right where she wanted me. I fell to the floor, and she straddled my face, riding my tongue as she bent over to devour my dick. We consumed and enjoyed tasting each other and got more excited.

I smacked her ass and motioned her to get off of my face. I was ready to fuck her until my dick gave out. I lay her on the carpet, pulled her legs toward me, and then spread them apart before sliding inside of her.

As I entered her, she gasped, grabbing my wrist. I threw slow, hard strokes in and out, giving her every inch of me. Moments later, I pushed her legs back and sped up my pace. As I felt her pussy tighten against my dick, she moaned louder, and the throbs of her pussy increased, so I knew she was about to come for me. But I wasn't ready for either one of us to release yet.

I pulled out and turned her over. She arched her back and spread her ass cheeks, giving me a perfect view of that pussy from the back. I just gazed at her beauty, thinking about how we would be spending the rest of our lives together, how much I loved her, and how much I loved how she made me feel in every way. Before reentering her from behind, I kissed her from the back of her neck, all the way down, then opened her ass cheeks, eating her ass, then down to her pussy.

All I could hear was her moans and her yelling, "Fuck." At one point, she was trying to run because it was too good, and she could barely take any more. Before I allowed her to come on my tongue, I rammed my dick inside of her. With one hand on the wall and one hand on her waist, I thrust as hard and fast as I could. Reneece let out a scream of pleasure as she came all over my dick.

I stroked her harder and spanked her ass in between soft, sweet whispers telling her how much I loved her, and it only intensified the atmosphere. Her pussy throbbing on my dick made me close to exploding. Reneece rubbed on her tender clit while my dick dug deep inside, reaching her G-spot.

"Mmm, fuck. Baby, I'm coming," she screamed.

"I'm coming in my pussy, OK, baby? Can I come inside of you? Please let me come inside of you," I begged as my grip tightened on the sheets. I was going to explode in her sea.

Reneece dug her nails deeper into my back and bit me on my chest before she screamed out my name, squirting her juices all over me. I knew I should've pulled out, but she felt so good on my dick. I moaned loudly before allowing my kids to find their way into her beautiful pink ocean.

After catching our breaths, I pulled out slowly and lay beside her on the carpet. "You're going to give me a heart attack at an early age fuckin' me like that," I said, kissing and rubbing her thighs.

Reneece laughed. "Why do you always ask or say you wanna come in me, like I'ma tell you no."

"I don't know," I said, with a chuckle.

Reneece turned over on her right side so she could face me. "I have to tell you something."

I rose and asked, "Besides how much you love me?"

Chortling, she said, "You know I love you, but no, there's something else."

Bringing her body into my arms, I asked, "What's that, babe?"

"I'm . . ." She was shortening her sentences, seemingly timid about telling me what was on her mind.

Kissing on her neck, I said, "You're what? Beautiful?"

"No, I'm pregnant. . . ." Reneece's eyes smiled at me. I couldn't be more excited and nervous for both of us.

Chapter 11

Reneece

"You're pregnant?" Eric asked, full of excitement. "Like . . . There's a little us swimming around in there?"

Tittering as Eric was rubbing my stomach, I said, "I blame you and the way you be fuckin' me."

Laughing out loud, he questioned, "How you gonna blame me? You be fuckin' me just as good."

"You kept nutting in me, knowing I wasn't on birth control," I said, playfully throwing a pillow at him.

He moved his hand from my belly down to my pussy. "Because you know that pussy had me like, 'Oh my God. What did you expect?'" he guffawed.

"See, you're fuckin' crazy. *That's* how we got here in the first place," I said, laughing at him.

We were play fighting when Eric pulled me close, pinching and kissing my cheek. "This is the best and biggest gift you could've ever given me. I love you so much."

"I love you more, Eric. I'm so excited. We're gonna have a baby." I smiled at him before laying my head on his bare chest and falling asleep.

A Week Later

Eric was getting ready to go to graduation practice when he received a phone call from the police department. He denied the call, so whoever was calling left a voicemail.

"Babe, you should've answered it. What if it was important?" I asked him while we were getting dressed.

"Well, they left a voicemail, so I can listen to it later," he replied nonchalantly as he pulled his belt through the loops on his jeans.

"No, we listen to it now," I insisted.

"Okay, fine," he said, breathing heavily.

Eric set the phone on the counter, playing the message through the speaker so we could both hear it. And the message said:

This is Detective Peterson. Dareen was able to post bail. A protective order has been placed for both you and Reneece. And, Eric, remember what we talked about. It'll work out. Just remember, if she does come near you guys, call 911 immediately.

I started to worry. "Eric, if she's out, she may really try to come for us again. What about our baby?"

"Shhh. You know I will not let anything or anyone harm you or our child. Now, I'll reach out to the detective on the way to practice, and you enjoy your girls' day with your fam. Everything is gonna be fine." He kissed my forehead before heading out of our bedroom.

While Eric decided to go to practice, I thought I would share the baby news with my mom and little sister. We headed to South Park Mall to do some shopping.

"You look mighty happy, Miss Lady," my mother told me as she took her ice cream cone from the cashier at Chick-fil-A.

"Yeah, Momma, she does look like she got a little glow on her," Francesca, my little sister, chimed in.

I chuckled at them. "Well, you are right. I have something to tell you both." We walked toward the mall's east wing, and my sister got sidetracked by some shoes displayed in front of Charlotte Russe.

"Momma, can I have these?" she begged, holding up a pair of tan boots with a four-inch heel.

"I just got you some shoes, girl," my mother said, tapping her thigh.

"So, what do you have to tell us?"

We continued to walk past different stores. "Well, I wanted to tell you—" I couldn't finish my statement because I could see through the glass someone was following us.

As the person got closer, I realized it was Dareen. She smiled at me, reaching for her back pocket. I knew that girl wasn't dumb enough to bring a loaded gun into a packed mall. We were approaching Aldo when we heard someone yell, "Gun!"

Dareen began shooting everywhere. She pushed people out of the way, trying to get to me. Her 9 mm aimed at me, and I tried to shove my sister and mother into the store out of harm's way, but it was too late. Dareen shot at us, and then my mother fell to the ground. Then she fired another round of bullets. I turned, looking for my sister. Francesca was lying, shaking on the floor, her blood quickly covering the tiles.

I started to pull my mother and sister into the store one by one while trying to escape Dareen before she killed us all. Out of my peripheral, I saw her approaching quickly. She cocked her gun, aiming it toward me as she came closer.

I got my sister and mother into the doorway of the store. Francesca tried to speak, but as she did, blood spilled out of her mouth. My mother was holding her side, trying to move closer to us, but she passed out.

Unable to keep my eyes off my family, I shouted, "Someone, help me! Someone, help us! Please!"

One of the store associates yelled out from the counter. "Ma'am, is everything okay? Are you hurt?"

I saw my mother and sister bleeding out in the middle of the floor in the store as I tried to figure out how to help them both. Then a white male came rushing to our aid. He pulled off his suit jacket to help control my sister's bleeding as I held my mother. "Someone, help us! Call 911, please, someone, please!" I cradled my mother as she lost consciousness again. My sister's body looked so lifeless.

As soon as the paramedics arrived, they rushed my sister and mother to Duke Hospital. I rode in the ambulance with them, watching the paramedics' every move. We arrived at Duke within minutes. I tried following them to the operating room, but they had a nurse escort me to the waiting room.

I called Eric once we arrived, letting him know what happened. I could barely speak. He just asked which hospital and said he was on the way. Twenty minutes had passed, and there was still no word from the doctors. I was pacing the floor when Eric rushed in.

Inspecting my body, he saw the huge bloodstain in the middle of my white shirt. "Are you hurt? Is the baby okay? Where's Francesca and Momma?"

Snapping at him, I said, "Get away from me—right now! I don't even want to see your ass now—maybe ever!"

Refusing to just leave me alone, he followed behind me. "Babe, calm down. We have to wait for the doctors to let us know something."

Increasing the volume in my tone, I said, "Calm down? *Calm down?* My mother and sister are on a fuckin' operating table because of you!"

He gently caressed my hand and said, "Babe, we will make it through this. I know everything will be fine."

"No," I said, yanking my hand from him. "This—all of this—it's *your* fault. You had to cheat on me. Cheat on me with a crazy bitch who just tried to fucking kill me in broad fucking daylight in a mall. She gave zero fucks about innocent bystanders. Now, look who's still suffering!" My hands were all in his face, trying to maintain my emotions.

"Reneece, please, you have to know I never wanted any of this to happen. I love you and your family as if they were my own." He attempted to pull me toward him.

"Get away from me! You may love them, hell, you may love me, but that doesn't fix the fact that I have two of my closest family members on operating tables right now 'cause you couldn't keep that piece of shitty dick in your fucking pants." I pushed him away to find a seat in the waiting room. I just needed space.

One of the doctors approached us slowly. He resembled Dr. Avery from *Grey's Anatomy*. He had a light complexion with a freckled face and blueish gray eyes. He walked over with three other surgeons, removing their face masks. "Ms. Moore?" he called out.

Standing up, I answered, "Yes, how's my mother? My sister? Are they okay?" I probed, walking toward them.

The doctor was hesitant with his answer, looking at his colleagues. He then went on to give us the news. "I'm so sorry, Ms. Moore. But we were unable to stop the bleeding and stabilize her in time. I'm so sorry, ma'am, but we lost her."

"Lost who? My sister? My mother? Who could you not save? *Answer* me," I screeched, trying to hold back my tears.

"Your mother is stable for now. We were able to remove the bullet before it could do too much damage, but she's lost a lot of blood. We will keep monitoring her and do everything we can," the male doctor said, stopping and taking a deep breath.

"My sister?" I asked, shifting my weight back and forth.

"Your sister, Miss Moore. Unfortunately, we were unable to save her. We did everything possible to stop the blood loss. But your sister had two bullets inside of her. One bullet hit her shoulder and went straight through her. But the fatal bullet that killed her pierced her heart.

There was only so much time we had. I'm so sorry for you and your family's loss." He reached his hand out, placing it on my shoulder.

My heart ached. My world was shattering right before my eyes. I screamed and screamed, but nothing was easing my pain. Eric attempted to pick me up and hold me, but this was all his fault. My tears were flowing, and the tighter he held me, the more I pushed away.

"No! No! This is your fault! *Your* fault!" I screamed, punching him in the gut.

"Reneece, baby. Come here. I'm so sorry," he said remorsefully, his eyes glossy as if he was going to shed a tear.

"You're sorry? You're fucking *sorry?*" I shouted, still hitting him, letting my tears and anger overpower me.

While I was crying, one of the doctors came back into the lobby area. "Miss Moore, if you and your fiancé are ready, I can take you back to your sister and mother."

"Thanks, Doc. Can you just give us a second, please?" Eric said. She nodded before walking away to give us a moment.

He was attempting to console me, but it wasn't working. Looking at him with disgust, I said to him, "Dareen killed my sister, and my mother is in there fighting for her life. You better do something about that bitch—or *I* will. You hear me, Eric? This was the last straw."

I got back up when I saw the doctor approaching. I wanted to punch Eric for allowing this disease into our lives. Yes, Dareen is a disease that must be cured. I left him sitting in the lobby to figure out his next move. If he doesn't have a solution by the time I get home, I'll have one for him.

Dear Diary,

She's gone. How will I be able to move on? My mother is laid up in a hospital bed, and my little sister is dead. No one will be able to make this feel normal to me. I watched her eyes close in my arms. But I didn't think she was leaving me, or it would be the last time I could hold her.

I don't think anyone could ever imagine this emptiness I'm feeling right now. Why the hell is he calling me? I wish he would just fucking stop! I wish everyone would stop calling. How do I tell my father that Eric's fling killed my little sister and left my mom in the hospital, fighting for her life? How does this benefit any of us?

I promise, Francesca, if you can hear me or see these words I'm writing, your death won't be in vain. I don't give a fuck if I must kill that bitch myself. She's mine.

What if Momma doesn't make it? Who supposed to help me prepare for this child? My mom is supposed to be here to help me celebrate graduation, pick my wedding dress, all this stuff that's happening, but instead, I'm waiting to see if she's gonna make it. . . . Or not.

I'm breaking down. I should be stronger than this. Why didn't God save my sister? He could've spared her. Why won't he take that ho instead? I hope the police get that ho before I do.

Reneece

Chapter 12

Dareen & Eric

I dropped Reneece off at our apartment. She wouldn't even look at me when she exited the car. I know she isn't the same beautiful-hearted person after this. Her baby sister is dead, and I couldn't bring her back. I just wanted to hold her, but she wanted nothing to do with me, so I gave her some space while I tried to figure out how to get rid of Dareen for good.

Reneece approached the driver's side of the car, banging on the window. I let it down slowly, not sure if she was going to kiss or hit me. "Eric, you tell her I'm coming for her. It wasn't my sister's time, and my mother is fighting for her fucking life. It's going to be her time soon. She wanted to play God. Now I'ma play God. And I won't miss."

I puckered up to kiss her, but she backed away. "Babe, I got this. I have to get to the police station and talk to the detectives. I promise I will make sure she will be put in a cell or a grave."

Snickering while she rolled her eyes at me, with her hands on her hips, she said, "Yeah, well, let them know if they did their job in the first place, my mom would still be here. And if they don't handle it correctly this time, I will—with or without their help."

"Babe!" I shouted to her, but she turned her back to me.

She didn't say another word. She just threw up her hands and slammed the door behind her. I pulled out of the driveway. I was going to meet with Detective Peterson, but I decided to meet with one of my homies who lived in the hood first.

I met my homie Jasper at Phoenix Crossing around seven that night. He was parked in front of the hair salon, bumping some Jeezy in his candy-red Cadillac DeVille sitting on twenty-fours.

Pulling up next to him, I slowly rolled my window down. "Yo, Jas!"

"Waddap, fool?" Opening the door with a blunt in his hand, he got out.

I got out of my car to dap him up. "What's going on, brother?" I asked him, leaning on my driver-side door.

"Shit, my nigg, you tell me. I heard y'all was at the police station." Lifting the blunt to his lips, he took a pull.

"Yeah, that's why I'm here. I need a way to protect my girl and me if the police don't keep this bitch, Dareen, locked up. She gonna try to kill us." I tossed my head back, looking up at the sky.

"So, what's up with that chick, man?" He handed the blunt to me.

Taking my hit off the blunt, I replied, "She won't let me go. Keep saying we meant to be and all that fuck shit. I moved away, transferred schools, and changed my number. Man, me and Reneece should be planning our wedding, and here we are, dealing with this dumb shit. You know she followed Reneece today and killed her sister and shot her mom's? Man, I just don't know how to get rid of her or make this right."

Jasper shook his head. "Damn, man. Tell li'l sis I send my condolences. But you right; you do got a problem. I can help you get some protection. I'll make sure the price is right. Let me make a few calls, and I can get you a strap or two. Stay by your phone, a'ight?"

"Word? Thanks, man." Giving Jasper a brotherly hug, I said, "Let me know when shit is ready."

"Bet. Stay by yo' phone, yo." Jasper entered his car as I did mine.

I was sitting in my car before pulling off, and I couldn't get my baby out of my mind. I needed to make sure she knew I would take care of her.

Me: Hey, baby, I just wanted to check on you.

Reneece: Yeah, well, I'll see you when you get home.

Me: Listen, I'm in the works with Jasper to create a plan B in case the detectives can't help.

Reneece: Cool.

Me: Babe—

Reneece: See you later, Eric

I sent several texts to her, but she left them unread. I departed from the small shopping center going toward the police station. Hopefully, they'll have a plan, and Dareen will be in custody.

Dareen

I was taken down to the police station. I ran from them at first and almost got away until one of them cut me off at the entrance. They gave me one choice: live and go down to the station, or they would shoot me where I stood. As much as I wanted to run, I figured they wouldn't hold me for long.

Once at the station, I saw two men in suits waiting for me. The first one said his name was Detective Oceanis, and the other introduced himself as Detective Peterson. They instructed this one officer, who was quite attractive with his albino skin and beautiful light brown eyes . . . He was to die for. Well, Detective Oceanis told him to take me to one of the interviewing rooms before he redirected his energy to a different cop, cussing him out

"So, what's your name?" I questioned him.

He cleared his throat, holding my arm. "My name is Officer Johnson."

I put on a performance. I cracked my voice as if I were going to cry. "Where are you taking me?"

"To an interview room, unless they say otherwise." Keeping his eyes straight ahead, he made minimal conversation with me.

Trying to keep him engaged and attempting to play on his heartstrings, I said, "That detective is so rude. Did you see how he talked to that other guy? Don't you think that was a little much?"

He cut his eyes at me. "He was just doing his job, ma'am."

"Yeah, I guess," I uttered as we continued to walk down the hallway.

I had to find a way out of that station. Regardless of what just transpired, I had unfinished business. Just the thought of that bitch running around playing victim, especially around Eric, made my blood boil. As we were walking, I eyed a bathroom ahead of us. I figured if I could get in there, there could be a window inside it I could use to escape.

Clenching my legs together, I asked, "Can I use the bathroom?"

He started looking around for help. "Let me get a female officer to be with you."

Side-eyeing him seductively, I said, "You can't watch me?"

"No, ma'am," he replied, still holding my arm.

I implored, "Please, I really have to go."

Officer Johnson contemplated, but the more I squirmed and acted like I was going to pee all over myself, he finally complied.

"Make it fast." He walked me into the bathroom, guiding me to one of the stalls. "Don't take forever."

Lewdly, I asked him, "Can you help me get my pants off?"

"No," he stated hardheartedly.

"Please? I'm handcuffed. So, either you can help me or uncuff me."

Officer Johnson refused to touch any part of my clothes. To refrain from undressing me, he uncuffed both of my hands. I could sense he was uncomfortable with me.

Facetiously, I asked, "Are you gay?"

He snorted his nose up at me. "Excuse me?"

Flippantly, I asked, "Are you gay? You seem very uncomfortable."

He sucked his teeth. "*This* is uncomfortable. Just pee, damn." He slowly closed the door to the stall.

"You don't like pussy, huh?" I teased before unbuttoning my pants and slowly squatting over the toilet to pee.

"Listen, I ain't gay. I'm doing my job. Now, hurry up."

Why not tease him a bit? I thought. I spread my legs as I sat on the bathroom seat and began to rub on my clit.

As he heard my soft moans, he opened the bathroom stall, keeping his head turned so he wouldn't look at me. "If you done, you need to get dressed—now."

"You wanna fuck me first then?" I provoked him, hoping it would work.

I could hear the aggravation in his voice. "No, I don't. Shit. What the hell is wrong with you?"

"The bulge in your pants says differently." Widening my smile with a titter, I pulled my pants and panties back up before exiting the stall.

Officer Johnson was very smart. I spotted his phone on record while we were in the bathroom. Now, I would devise a quick scheme to get his phone and leave the station. I stood there after washing my hands, watching him stare at me through the mirror, thinking of different plans, but none seemed worth trying. When I was about to try something different, a female officer appeared.

Looking relieved, he looked back at his fellow officer. "Hey, there, Joan. You got it from here?"

She glanced at me with her short, blimp-shaped body and sneered at me. "I sure do."

Leaving me in the middle of the bathroom floor, he said, "Perfect."

She held the bathroom door open slightly and never took her eyes off me. She said, "Detective Peterson is waiting, and he wanted to talk to you first."

Smirking at the fellow officer, he said, "Cool. I'll let you take it from here."

Joan waited for Officer Johnson to leave before pushing me into the middle stall. The bathroom stall smelled of vomit and shit. I thought about playing the victim with her. Flip the script on Officer Johnson to get him in trouble and make her feel sorry for me. But unfortunately, I learned that it wasn't going to work.

"Thank God you came in when you did. He was trying to get me to fuck him. Saying it was a fantasy of his," I exaggerated.

"Yeah, I find that hard to believe. See, you have been causing my big sis from my sorority a lot of problems, and Officer Johnson is *my* man. And I know my man. If he did want to cheat, it wouldn't be with a loose pussy skank like you." Slamming the door to the stall, she left me by myself.

I could overhear her conversing with someone, but I couldn't tell who. I hoped Eric was coming to my rescue like I knew he would. But the closer the voice got to the stall they had me locked in, I knew it wasn't him. It was the bitch I meant to kill today. Reneece. She slowly opened the stall, and our eyes locked.

I sat there with my resting bitch face. "Well, how lucky can I be? Is my future husband here too?" I teased.

Reneece said nothing as she walked toward me. She wore a black tank top, black tights, and black boots. Before she got close to me, she pulled a pair of gold brass knuckles from her bra. I was still handcuffed when Reneece threw her first punch, aiming straight for my gut.

In between punches, I muttered, "You can only beat me 'cause I'm handcuffed."

"Oh, you think that's why I'm able to beat that ass? Okay." Reneece took me by the neck of my scooped-neck T-shirt and threw my body into the sink.

"Uncuff her since she wanna talk that shit!"

Her little officer friend, Joan, obliged to her request. My hands were now free, but I wasn't able to land a punch before she was back punching me in my chest. Pushing back, I squared up, preparing myself for this fight. Her friends were cheering her on in the background.

I grabbed her face, digging my nails into her pretty little face. I clawed her face, leaving scratch marks all over it. Reneece yelled, "Bitch," as she felt the sting from the scratches.

She continued to hit me harder and harder. I could even taste my own blood in my mouth. Joan let her get in a few more rounds until she made me fall to my knees before telling Reneece to stop.

Breathing heavily, she said to me, "If they let you out, on my mother and dead little sister's life, you will *never* see another day 'cause I *will* find you."

She acted as if she were Rocky or Mike Tyson. She kept jumping up and down, beating her fist into her palm.

Leering at her, I said, "Well, we'll both be dead 'cause you can't have him. I'll die first."

"That can be arranged." She tried to attack me again, but one of her friends stopped her. As her friends held her back from swinging on me, she taunted me. "Yeah, well, I do have him and always will. Oh, by the way, we're having a baby, you miserable bitch."

Before walking out of the bathroom, Reneece approached me once more and spit in my face, then kicked me in my stomach. I looked up at her, my eyes full of rage. I wanted her to feel my anger deep in her soul. Her officer friend, Joan, handcuffed me again while I was lying on the floor. She picked me up and led me from the bathroom to another office, leaving me there to plot my revenge on all of them.

I waited inside the office while Joan and some other officers gossiped about me in front of the door. Moments later, a short Hispanic man came walking into the room. He took one look at me, then had one of the officers take me from the office.

"Where are you taking me?" I said, laughing as I walked.

"I'm Detective Peterson. And to answer your question, Dareen, to have a conversation, just us two," he said as he looked down at his phone, moving to the side of the hall. "Keep going, I'm right behind you," he instructed.

The male officer who was escorting me seemed to be a middle-aged white guy. His skin was red and chaffed, like he had been in the sun too long.

"Come on, girl, keep goin'."

"Yeah, I am gonna keep goin' 'cause no one can stop me. Or me and Eric from being together," I shouted, letting out a short devilish chuckle behind it.

Detective Peterson walked behind me. "If I were you, I would stop laughing. You're in some serious shit, Miss Lady."

The officer who escorted me into this dark room with no windows threw me on a hard, silver, lawn-looking chair. "Hey, I did nothing wrong," I stated boldly.

He closed the steel door behind him to the integration room. "Oh yes, you did. You killed someone with your crazy antics this afternoon at the mall."

I shook my head in disbelief, my smile suddenly fading away. "What? What did you say?"

He placed a toothpick into his mouth. "Yes, a murder charge. A great rep for a young lady like you."

"Listen, you have this all wrong. Did you find the gun on me?" I asked, trying to figure out how they pinned it on me.

"There were enough witnesses who described you as the shooter." He waved his hand in front of the mirror, then the door opened, with two cops in the doorway.

"Take her away now, fellas."

Grabbing me from the chair, the two officers roughly handcuffed me. I couldn't believe what I was hearing. I was about to get a murder charge. If I'm going to catch a charge, especially for murder, it's going to be for killing Reneece. Her sister and mother were just collateral damage. It's their fault they were in the way. I can't go down like this. What will Eric do without me? I have to find a way out of this.

Chapter 13

Reneece & Eric

I departed from the police station around seven thirty that evening. As I was pulling off, Eric was pulling in. He honked at me to get my attention, but I kept going. My phone started playing his ringtone, "Flaws and All" by Beyoncé.

I answered the call after the third ring. "Yes, Eric?"

"I know you heard me honking at you."

"I didn't hear you," I lied.

"Reneece, I know you're mad at me and hurting. I am too, but don't push me away," he pleaded.

"You fucking hurting? Are you fucking kidding me? Who did you lose today? Huh, Eric?" I shouted at him.

He sighed deeply. "Reneece, that's not, you know, what I mean. Listen, I love you, all right? We will make it through this."

"I love you too, baby. Look, I gotta meet my father. I'll see you later."

Hanging up the phone, all these emotions flooded me at once. Punching my steering wheel as hard I could, I shouted, "Fuck," to help release some of my tension, but it didn't help as much as I thought it would.

I drove to my parents' home. My brother's car was pulling into the driveway in front of me. I parked beside his red Camaro. My brother looked at me as I got out of the vehicle. He waved through the window.

"You gonna get out or just sit there?" I asked through the window.

He held up his finger as to give him a minute, so I left him in the car and went inside the house. My father opened the door with open arms.

"Hey, Daddy," I said, embracing him tightly.

He kissed my cheek before releasing me from his hug. "Hey, baby girl."

"Donte's here. He's sitting in the car."

"Nah. Looks like he's leaving." My dad pointed at my brother's car backing up wildly.

From my father's doorstep, I yelled, "Where you going? Donte, where the fuck you goin'?"

He sped off down the street without answering me. I was going to call him, but my father took my phone.

"He'll be OK. Maybe something happened. I'm sure we'll see him at the hospital. Come on in. You wanna eat something?" he asked, placing his arm around my waist as we entered the home.

I shook my head as my father went into the kitchen to finish his dinner before we headed to the hospital. While he ate, I went into my sister's room. Her Trey Songz posters covered her wall, and her princess canopy bed was still mangled like she just got out of it. I sat on her bed and took one of her stuffed animals into my arms. I rocked back and forth as my tears flowed down my cheeks.

My father entered the room. "Reneece, honey," he said softly.

"Daddy, I should've protected them. I didn't see it coming. I'm so sorry, Daddy." I sobbed, leaning my head into his chest.

"Baby girl, you cannot blame yourself for what God has chosen to do. It's all a part of his plan." My father ran his hand through my hair.

He wiped my tears and looked at me. "I love you, Daddy," I said.

"I know, baby girl, I love you too. Let's go head to the hospital. Donte is already there. Davineece said she didn't want to come with us, so we can go ahead when you're ready, baby girl." He patted my leg before exiting the bedroom to get dressed.

"Daddy, you wanna ride with me, or you're going to drive yourself?" I questioned, sniffling my nose.

"It doesn't matter, baby. I'm sure to get home between you and your brother," he responded, grabbing a sweater from the closet near the front door.

We arrived at the hospital around thirty minutes later. My body was covered in chills as we approached the morgue. We decided to view and identify my sister's body before going to see my mom. My brother was standing at the window in front of the morgue, observing the bodies.

He turned around, seeing us coming up beside him. "Hey, sis, hey, Dad."

"Hey, Donte," I reached out for a hug, but he half-assed the hug.

Our father came in between us. "She looks so peaceful, doesn't she?" he asked.

"Yeah, I guess," I said, turning to hug him as I cried.

Holding me tightly, he said, "It will be okay. We'll get through this." He released his hold, then eyed Donte and me, saying, "There's something you two should know about your mother."

My brother and I looked at each other, then back at him, confused about what he would say.

"What you mean, Pop?" Donte asked, pushing himself in between me and our father.

Backing away from us, he asked, "Your mom didn't get to tell you guys?"

"Tell us what?" Donte replied.

He moved over to one of the benches available in the hallway. Exhaling slowly, he said, "Your mother was given four months to live. She has been battling cancer for over two years now. I thought she told you both. I begged her to inform you guys, but she said she wanted to tell you all when she felt it was right."

"I didn't even get to tell her I'm pregnant," I said, falling to the floor as I felt my heart sink to the pit of my stomach.

"Pops, so you telling me, with or without Mom being shot, she's gonna die soon anyway?" Donte's voice was shaking as his lips quivered.

Lowering his head, he answered. "They found a tumor on the left side of the brain. She refused any surgery or treatment. She said God will do his will. So, she wanted to see both of y'all and tell you guys personally. She also wished that if she ended up on any life support, we don't linger her process. She's ready to go."

"Well, I ain't fucking ready, Dad. Neither is Neece. How are we supposed to be ready? Shit, Neece just said she's having a baby," Donte yelled, then paused. The two of them stopped, watching my reaction.

"Neece, baby, I'm going to be a grandpa?" my father asked, leaning over toward me.

"Mm-hmm. That's what I was going to tell Mommy and Fran today but never got the chance to." I started to wail, thinking of everything. It was killing me.

As I continued to snivel, my brother and father came to me. We consoled one another, sitting in the morgue hallway.

Eric

I was at the police station for at least two hours. I provided them statements of how Dareen came into my life and how things ended up so fucked up. I knew that by her just having killed someone, she was going to go down for murder. I watched the interview between her and Detective Peterson, and she seemed so unbothered. She didn't care about killing Francesca.

After watching the interview, they moved me into the lobby to wait for the detective as they booked her and placed her in county jail. Detective Peterson emerged to speak with me. We walked back to his office to talk privately.

"So that's it, right? We won't have to worry about her anymore?" I asked as I sat down.

"Well, you're not out of the woods yet. She has no record or anything. So I'm sure within a week or so, they'll try to give her a bond hearing, and then there will be court, more so a trial." He took his toothpick out of his mouth, throwing it into the trash can beside his desk.

"So what the fuck are you saying to me? My fiancée and the baby she's carrying still aren't safe? If that bitch can even get a bail hearing and they grant it to her, she's able to roam free?" Jumping out of the chair, I slammed my fist on the desk.

"Eric, it's not up to me. I've done everything on my end. I'll even talk to the DA, but there are no guarantees. I just have to be honest with you up front so there are no surprises." He leaned back in his chair, looking at me like a concerned father who had raised me. "Listen, regardless of what does or doesn't happen, please keep us informed and always feel free to reach out, young man."

"Yeah, whatever." I turned my back and walked out of his office.

While preparing to leave the station, Reneece's brother sent me a text asking me to meet him for a drink at Carolina Ale House. I knew he wanted to talk about today, and if he didn't try to kill me when I showed up,

I would be shocked. I sent him a message back, letting him know I was leaving the police station and was on my way.

I walked into the Ale House and saw him at the bar, so I approached him. "Aye, bro, what's up, man? I'm happy you called me out here."

Donte's face was as cold as ice. His eyes were filled with pain and hatred.

"Aye, yo. It's been a long week," he said with a heavy groan.

"Yeah. How you holding up?" I asked, extending my hand to his.

He sat in the wooden chair by the bar, dissing my handshake. "As good as I'm going to be. You want a drink?"

I placed my varsity jacket on the back of my chair and replied, "Uhhh, yeah, a shot of Cîroc Red Berry."

Donte smiled at the tall, light-skinned bartender. She batted her eyes at him, leaning all over the counter, placing her large breasts in his face as he placed our drink orders. She said she would be right back, giving us time to talk.

Watching the bartender pour up the shots, he asked, "You talked to my sister?"

"Not since earlier. I texted her, letting her know we would be out, and I was coming home right after. But she never responded," I said before taking my first shot.

He said, "We just found out Moms has cancer. So even if that bitch didn't kill her, man, she ain't got long, and our little sister . . . You know?" he sniffled as he fought back the tears.

I was shocked to hear the news. "What? You serious? Damn, man."

Nodding slowly, he said, "Yeah, you heard me right. Shit's fucked up."

"Yeah, man." Donte took another double shot of Henny to the head. "So, yo' crazy-ass, ex-side bitch tried to kill Reneece but killed Francesca and shot our mom instead."

"I'm handling it," I told him so he knew I wasn't taking any of this lightly. "I love your sister, you know that. I am so sorry for what happened today, and I won't allow that bitch to fuck up anything else in our lives."

Donte took a sip of his Corona. "You know we have to protect her. A crazy bitch like that will not stop."

I signaled the bartender to come over so I could order another shot. "If they ever release her from jail and she comes anywhere near your sister, Dareen is gone. That's a fact."

He took a double shot of Crown Royal, and we made small talk while watching television. Donte was more distant toward me than ever before. Just like Reneece, I knew he was blaming me for Francesca's death. I was about to order something to eat when breaking news came across the screen.

Reporting live at Durham County Jail. Officers are looking for a female suspect, Dareen J. Jacobs. Police are saying she is dangerous and at large. She may also be armed. I will be back later at ten with more details as they emerge. Durham County Police and the sheriff's office are asking if you have seen or have any information on Dareen's whereabouts, please get in touch with crime stoppers at 919-555-6605.

I looked at Donte and said, "Listen, regardless of how you may feel about me right now, we have someone to protect that we both love. We have to get to Reneece."

Donte's eyes were glued to the TV screen. "What the fuck, man? How the hell is she even free?"

I placed forty dollars on the bar under my shot glass. "Yo, I'm out. I'm not going to let her hurt Reneece or our unborn child."

Donte swallowed his last shot, then faced me. "I'm right with you, bro. We gotta get to her before Dareen. Ain't shit happening to my sister."

Chapter 14

Dareen

I couldn't believe it worked. Men are so fucking dumb. If they can get the pussy, they'll take it, no questions asked. While in my holding cell, I met one of the patrolling officers on duty that night. After a few winks and whispers, he finally played into my hand. He took me into one of the empty offices in the jail and fucked me right on top of the empty desk. While we were fucking, I asked him for help getting out of a situation that I was being framed for.

The officer was named Tyshawn. He was about 23, nice, with smooth, purple chocolate skin and pearly whites. He was something beautiful to look at and fuck. After a twenty-minute quickie, he told me to wait in there while he took a nap. I waited to make sure he was completely knocked out, then crept up to grab his keys to the jail's doors. Carefully watching my step and surroundings, I made it to one of the back doors.

Not knowing how much time I had, I ran until I could barely breathe. I saw a cop car zooming down the street and quickly hid behind a dumpster near a shopping center. To my surprise, I wasn't the only one hiding. A bum was beside me in his dusty, torn Carolina Panthers shirt and cut-up sweatpants.

This bum smelt like rotting raw chicken that had been left out for months. His teeth were way beyond yellow, and he was missing the whole front row on the bottom. I asked him if he had a phone or a way for me to get to Briar Creek.

Nodding slightly, he pulled out a cheap, prepaid phone and said I could take it only if he got a little something, and as crazy as it sounds, I needed him. I had to be able to reach someone, especially being on the run. So I agreed. I informed him that he would not be fucking me, but he could jack off on my tits.

With an expansive smile, he unzipped his pants, and as he did, dirt and dust flew everywhere from it, some even getting in my eyes.

"I haven't bust a nut in four years. My wife left me because I spent all our money on crack, and I couldn't get no pussy since then. So I need this," he expressed.

"Yeah, that's cool. Let's do this." I motioned, lifting my orange shirt over my head, revealing my perky 42-C cup breasts.

His dick was very skinny and looked dirtier than him. I pinched my nipples and juggled my boobs, giving him some visual. The sound of him jacking his dick sounded like someone was starting a fire. It took him about ten minutes to bust his nut. Soon, he lay behind the dumpster, shivering as he released his sperm all over his chest. I picked up his phone while he rearranged himself.

Knowing I was wanted, I had to find a safe haven. I tried calling my father, but I got no answer. I even tried calling one of my sisters, but she didn't fucking answer. The only place I could think of going was Joanna's. The bum I fucked to get the phone also had about forty dollars on him. He gave it to me, telling me to be safe tonight. He must've thought I was a prostitute or something because he also told me he was gonna try to get some more money and to come back and see him.

I left downtown and caught a free taxi ride to Briar Creek area where Joanna stayed. When we arrived at her apartment complex, I asked the driver to drop me off at the clubhouse. Then I walked down to her townhome and saw her bedroom light on. I knocked on her door, but no answer. I hollered her name, but still no damn answer. I went to the back of the townhome, where she had a small backyard area and back door. I took some of the gravel and rocks from the parking lot and threw them at her window.

After all my attempts to get her to wake up when unanswered, I thought of another plan. I couldn't stand outside her door for too long, especially if a neighbor or the security in her complex saw me. It wasn't a risk I was willing to take. I stepped away from her door and went around the back door. I remembered where she told me she placed her spare key.

I searched through the short bush beside her back door, feeling for a small plastic rock. Her neighbor's light came on, and I could hear a car approaching. Before anyone could see me, I found it. I removed the black and gray fake rock, revealing the extra house key. I ran to her front door, keeping it balled up in my fist.

I opened the door as quietly as possible. All her lights were off. The only light on was a candle that seemed to be burning for quite some time. I tiptoed up the stairs, hoping she would be asleep so I could take her car keys and some clothes. But the closer I got to the top of her stairs, I understood why she didn't hear me outside.

Her bedroom door was wide open, and I saw my friend riding some man's dick. She was all into it. Her head was tossed back, his hands were on her titties, and she rode him in perfect rhythm. She yelled to the top of her lungs that she was coming when he told her to stop so he could get it from behind.

As he grunted and panted like a dog, he said, "You're a nasty-ass bitch. Yeah, you love this fuckin' dick, right? Tell daddy you love this fucking dick."

"Yes, yes, I love daddy's dick. Mmmm-hmmmm . . . Fuuuucccckkkk," she moaned, and it sounded so sexy to my ears. How soft it sounded in between her gasps for air.

He slapped Joanna on the ass and pulled her hair back like it was a harness. I couldn't tell if he saw me when he looked out into the hallway. But I definitely was watching how roughly he thrust inside of her as she held her pink satin covers.

Now, from what I could see at the top of the stairs, he wasn't all that cute, but shit, neither was Joanna's ass. He reminded me of an uglier, younger version of that rapper, Ice Cube. But his stroke game was on point. The way he was fucking her from the back was making my pussy wet. If I were into that kinky shit, I would've joined them just to see if he was as good as they made it seem.

I watched them for a few minutes, then I groped my tits, pinched my nipples, and my pussy began throbbing for some of that action. Slowly and quietly, I slipped off my jailhouse pants, slipped my hand into my panties, and masturbated. After I got my nut, I sucked the cum off three of my fingers. That nut was precisely what I needed to help keep my head in the game.

I was proud to see how sexy and good my girl was taking that dick. But my situation was more critical, so I thought I would make my presence known.

Clearing my throat from within the dark shadows of the hallway, I clapped my hands, saying, "Damn, bitch, you be taking that dick, huh? I'm proud of you."

"What the hell?" the male exclaimed, quickly pulling his dick out of her.

Joanna's eyes widened like she saw a ghost. She asked, "What the hell are you doing here?"

I attempted to make puppy dog eyes to make her feel sorry for me. "I need your help. I had to come to you. You're my best friend."

"Nah, babe, it's OK. She'll be gone soon." Joanna turned to her friend, who was in bed with her, holding his hand. "How the hell did you get inside my house?" she asked.

Joanna looked so surprised to see me. She must've forgotten about showing me where her spare key was. I sat on her carpet, watching her cover herself up. I couldn't believe how she was acting toward me. She was the only friend I truly had left.

Sitting on the floor near her bedroom door, I said to her, "You were supposed to be my friend."

Staring straight ahead at her TV as it played *Belly*, she said, "I was . . . 'til you decided to threaten and beat me, so how do you think we're still friends? Or even cool?"

"You called me crazy," I exclaimed, slamming my fist into her floor.

Slapping her hands on the bed, she said, "Because you *are*. Look at you. How the hell did you even get out of jail?"

With a snort and a quick roll of my eyes, I replied, "Using my womanly skills."

Joanna rolled out of her bed, exposing her naked body. "I want you out of my house."

Stepping into her bedroom doorway, I told her, "I need your car and some clothes."

"No. I'm not giving you shit. You need to go back to jail before they arrest all of us." Joanna picked up her phone and started calling someone.

Standing in her bedroom doorway, I asked, "Who the hell are you calling?"

Her chest swelled up. "Who the fuck do you think I'm calling?"

Bucking my chest up at her, I said, "Bitch, it bet not be the police. Or is that your new bestie, Reneece?"

She wouldn't answer me; she just kept talking on the phone. Joanna didn't understand that my paranoia was at an all-time high. I just wanted to talk and get her to help me. She was supposed to be my friend. Not worrying about her friend in the bed, I bum-rushed her, knocking the phone out of her hand. I tackled her to the ground and was pulling my arm back to punch her in the face when her friend grabbed me, trying to pull me away.

After I elbowed him in his eye, he released his hold on me. One of Joanna's heels was lying adjacent to the right side of us. I took the shoe and slapped her across her face. Her right eye began to bleed as I stuck her stiletto in it. Leaving her on the ground wailing about her eye, I went to finish off her friend. He was on the left side of the bed, grabbing his gun.

"You going to shoot me? If so, shoot me, nigga, or you too pussy?" I teased, standing in front of him, not afraid to die.

"Fuck, yeah, I'm gonna shoot you, crazy bitch." He pulled the trigger, but he forgot to take off the safety.

I used that to take my chance. "She always fucking with some dumb niggas. You can't even protect her—or yourself," I taunted.

Moving quickly, I grabbed the wooden sculpture from the nightstand and beat him in the head repeatedly until I saw blood drip from his skull. Dropping the statue on the ground, I focused back on Joanna.

"Where's my phone? I need my phone," she murmured.

I looked at her boyfriend on the ground, knocked out cold. With his gun in my hand, taking off the safety, I cocked the gun and shot him once in the abdomen. Joanna was crawling to her phone when I walked over to the opposite side of the bedroom. Her back was turned to me. She had no clue I was behind her; the gun was aimed directly at her back. She was placing her 911 call when I fired four rounds into her back.

She turned around, lying on her carpet. The operator was trying to get her attention. I ended the call without saying a word. Joanna was trying to move away from me, but I took hold of her ankles, keeping her near me. She kicked me in the face, which pissed me off.

"You stupid cunt," I shouted, straddling her. "I told you not to fuck with me." I placed my hands on her neck, and with every ounce of strength I had in me, I strangled her. I kept my hands around her neck until her eyes closed.

Kneeling down beside her body, I said, "I hated to do this to you. I loved you like a sister, you-you thot-ass bitch. I was never after you, but you chose the wrong side."

I ran my fingers through Joanna's hair before kissing her neck. As I kneeled beside her, I pushed the barrel of my gun into her stomach, firing two more rounds into her body. Making sure she would not survive, I waited to see if I could find a pulse. It was really faint, but it was fading.

Getting up from the floor, I walked over to her closet to grab some clothes to change into. I heard sirens approaching; I could hear them roaring from her upstairs window. I gathered what I could and made my way out of her home. Now it was time to complete what I intended to do in the first place: *kill Reneece.*

Chapter 15

Reneece

After leaving the hospital, I thought I would spend some time at Jalisa's house. She has always been my peace in any storm. I knew I could confide in her about everything that's happened today. I arrived at her apartment, noticing her lights were off, but her car was in the driveway.

After parking my car beside her silver Suzuki Forenza, I exited the vehicle and walked toward her front door, but something seemed a bit off. Usually, the porch light for her apartment would come on with any movement, but it never came on. I heard crunching sounds under my Air Force 1s, then noticed I was stepping on a floor covered with glass. Someone had busted open the small windows near her doorknob. I went to touch the doorknob, but the lock on the door had been broken, and it opened with a simple touch.

My phone started ringing in my purse. Ignoring the two calls back-to-back, I tiptoed my way into the house. I took my phone out of my purse to use as a flashlight as I continued to hear crunchiness under my feet. But before I could turn my flashlight on, my phone rang again.

"Hello," Eric's voice was tense, full of worry.

"Hey, babe, I'm at Jalisa's. It looks like someone broke in or something. There's glass everywhere." I told him as I walked through her apartment.

Eric screamed, "Get the fuck out of there! Get out of there *now*."

I was baffled about why he would want me to leave. "What? I wanna make sure she's okay 'cause her car is still here."

Eric got louder. "Get the fuck out of there *now*. Dareen broke out of fuckin' jail. Get out now, in case she's there."

Stopping in the middle of the floor, I couldn't believe what I was hearing.

"What? Are you sure?"

"Gotdamn it, Reneece. Yes, I'm sure. Your brother and I will meet you at the house. I'm sure she doesn't know where I'm at in Raleigh, but Durham is so fuckin' small, she could've followed you there, and we may not have known. So, leave, *please*," Eric pleaded, and even with his voice hard, it was still alarming.

"Okay, babe. I'm leaving now," I told him, turning back toward the front door.

"I'm staying on the phone with you until you're in the car. Nah, until you get here," he said, and I knew he was serious.

"Listen, I'm OK, and I want you to know that I lo—" I couldn't get my words out before a light came on in the sunroom.

"You, what? Reneece? Reneece, are you there?" Eric shouted.

"Yeah, I'm here. A light just came on, and I can hear a door opening," I whispered.

Walking softly and trying to avoid the glass on the floor, I quietly made my way to the room to ensure my girl was okay. Eric was still on the phone, and the closer I got, the more I could see. Her living room had been mangled. It looked like there was a brawl right there.

"Reneece, you're supposed to be getting in the car! What the fuck are you doing?" Eric questioned.

Putting the phone back to my ear, I said, "I think something happened here. I can't just leave her if she's hurt. She wouldn't do that to me," I gritted through my teeth.

"Fine, I'm on my way. I have to keep y'all safe. Do not hang up this phone until I get there. That's not a suggestion either," he demanded.

I was going to say okay when I peeped my head into the crack of the door, and there was my best friend. She was tied up with a black eye, a swollen lip, and a knot on her forehead. But Dareen looked just as bad. Jalisa tore her ass a new one. Dareen's right eye was swollen. It looked like her left leg was cut, but she bandaged it.

"Eric, I need to call you back," I said, hoping he would just hang up and come straight here.

"No, I'm staying on the phone. Are you still there?" Eric continued to talk to me, but I wasn't hearing him. I saw Dareen sitting there as if she knew I was there.

"Eric, just hurry up." I disconnected the call and went over to the main door to the sunroom.

Dareen saw me and sat up straight. "Well, well, nice for you to finally show up. I was starting to get bored."

I stepped into the sunroom, looking at my friend gagged and tied up. "Well, I'm here now. You can let her go." I stepped in. "You know you're one sick, crazy bitch."

"And if I am that crazy?" Dareen stood up and pointed a gun at her head.

"Whoa. What are you doing?" I asked, stepping closer to her.

Dareen said, "I'm crazy, right?"

I waited for her to blow her brains out, but the gun was empty.

"What's wrong with you? You act like you were done wrong," I exclaimed. "Do you realize what you've done? All this over someone who wants nothing to do with you," I shouted, walking closer to her.

"You walking up on me like you going to do something," Dareen said. "I'm not in jail or cuffed to a stall now."

"I'll fuck you up either way, bitch. Ain't nobody scared of you," I said, pulling my hair into a ponytail and removing my gold hoop earrings from my ears.

Dareen pulled a gun from behind her. I stood still in the middle of the floor. I wasn't sure what she was thinking. Tapping the weapon on her knee, she said, "You ready to die, heffa?"

"Are *you* ready to die?" I responded, holding my stance and blocking my friend from harm's way.

She placed the gun down by her feet, throwing her hands in the air. "What's up then?"

This is my chance, I thought. Jalisa was on the ground, struggling to get her hands free. Dareen was staring right at me, ready to charge me again. I stepped over Jalisa, picking up one of the unplugged lamps near the bookshelf Jalisa was sitting by. Dareen and I ran toward each other. With all my might, I swung that lamp across her face. She fell to the ground, her eyes closed, and she didn't move.

I hoped that hit was enough to knock her out for a bit. I kicked her with my foot, but she didn't move. I pulled Jalisa near the main entrance of the sunroom so I could get her untied.

I worked on freeing Jalisa's feet and legs from the ropes tying them. "When I get you untied, I want you to go get the police. Then find Eric."

My friend refused my request. "I'm not leaving without you. We can get her another day. Come up with a plan."

"Lisa, I need this all to end. She's killed my sister and left my mom in the hospital, fighting for her life. Her ass is mine." I finished untying my friend so she could escape and get help.

Jalisa looked up, observing the room. "Where the hell did she go? What if she went into my bedroom through that other door?"

I looked over, seeing that Dareen was no longer where I left her. "I don't know. Maybe she did and left. But that means you're safe now." I said, tossing the ropes on the other side of the room.

Jalisa looked around. "Look, let's grab your shit and go while we have the chance."

I shook my head. I had unfinished business. "Jalisa, you go. I'm canceling that bitch!"

"No, bitch, we're *both* leaving. I know you want revenge, but we need to handle it the right way." She took my hand, and together, we got off the floor.

We ran toward her front door. Jalisa was grabbing her keys when I heard the shots—*pow, pow.* I looked over my body and saw no wound. I looked behind me at Jalisa. She was on the ground.

"No!" I screamed, bending to her aid.

"Neece, go. I'll be fine. Go, now," she uttered with a tear falling from her eye. I placed my hand on her leg, where the two bullets went in. I was trying to compress the bleeding when Dareen grabbed my hair, dragging me into the living room.

She laughed sinisterly. "You aren't going anywhere. We aren't done yet, my dear."

She grabbed my phone out of my pocket. "Unlock the phone," she demanded.

"Fuck you," I said, clawing at her hands, trying to break free.

She slammed my head into the corner of the wooden coffee table Jalisa had in the middle of the floor. "Unlock it, or I kill you now."

Giving in, I unlocked my phone. She went through my text messages. "Oh, there's my sexy man. Now, I want you to smile. We're going to send him a picture."

"I'm not doing shit for you. Why won't you leave us alone?" I screamed, crying.

"You won't leave us alone," she said. "Now, smile, you aggravating-ass bitch."

She jerked my head back, placing her arm around my neck. Holding the phone out, she took our picture. She was smiling so hard, and I was in the picture looking terrified with a cut on my forehead from the table.

Dareen sent Eric a picture along with a text reading If you want to save her or your unborn child, meet us at the following location in an hour and come alone. Try anything crazy, Eric, and she won't make it to the location at all: no police, no family, no friends. Just us, like it always should've been.

The last thing I remember was her taking that picture and sending it to Eric. Then her arm tightened around my neck, and everything went dark.

Chapter 16

Eric

I was doing 95 mph on the highway, trying to get to Jalisa's house, when I got a text from Reneece. I looked down at my phone and saw a glimpse of the message. I got off at the South Park exit, pulled over at the Citgo gas station, and read the text.

The image of Reneece looking in total distress turned my stomach. I called her phone, but no one picked up. I screamed inside my car, hoping it would release some of the anger and tension. I called for the fifth time and still got no answer. Wishing they were still at Jalisa's house, I zoomed over there.

I crept into Jalisa's apartment complex and approached her building, but neither of their cars was outside. My heart was racing fast. I backed out of the parking lot and switched directions. I was going to go wherever that address led me when I finally heard my text notification go off.

Reneece: We aren't there, my little Eric pooh. I will let you know when we arrive at the location and when you are free to join us. Love always, Dareen. You can stop fuckin' callin' and no need to respond. Just wait. Xoxo (kissy smiley face emoji)

As much as I wanted to track and follow them, I had no clue what that ho had in mind. My heart was saying go, but my mind was telling me to be smart; that's the only way they could be saved. So, I decided to forward the text to Donte and the detective. The detective called me immediately.

"Yo!" I answered angrily.

"Eric, this is Detective Peterson. I'm going to have some of my guys meet you in Raleigh at your apartment, and also some of the best cops I trust from Raleigh PD. That way, we can cover all grounds." Then he gave me instructions that I wasn't giving a shit about.

"Listen, thanks for the help. But right now, my fiancée and child are in danger! I don't give a flying fuck about no cops or anybody else. I'm going to get my family." Not wanting to hear anything else he had to say, I disconnected the phone and tossed it on the passenger's seat.

I arrived at my home and found Donte waiting in my parking lot. If he wasn't going to kill me earlier, he definitely was now. Getting out of our cars simultaneously, he swung at me. His left hook landed on my jaw. I didn't fight back. With every jab he threw at me, I stood there and took it as I should have.

He went to throw one more hit when his father pulled up. "Donte, that's enough!" he shouted from the car.

Donte lowered his fists, looking at me before coming in to hug me as he wailed out for his family.

"Come on, let's go inside and talk," I insisted, walking beside him into my apartment.

Once inside with Reneece's father and Donte, I grabbed an ice pack from the freezer to put on my face in case it swelled.

"I'm sorry, bro. I just saw you and thought about my sisters, and I know you can't be everywhere, but I'm done losing family today, period." He went into my refrigerator and grabbed a Bud Light.

Someone knocked on the door as I was getting ready to tell them what I knew. I wasn't expecting anyone. We all looked at one another, not sure who it could be. I told his father to hide. Donte loaded and aimed his pistol, just in case it was Dareen. To our disappointment, it was Detective Peterson and a few cops.

"Hey, Eric. As I told you, there will be a few officers here for you all's protection until we can find Reneece and get her home to you and your family." Then the detective and his fellow officers walked into my apartment.

"No offense, Detective, but I'd rather be with the family right now. No cops. I can call you when y'all are needed," I responded, still holding my door open, hoping they would turn around and leave.

"Right now, we'll wait here for a bit and see what we can do or if we can find any leads." The detective and his comrades made themselves comfortable on my living room furniture.

Donte motioned for me to follow him up the stairs to talk privately. I shook my head, pointing to the kitchen for us to speak there.

"Yo, that bitch got my sister. We can't wait for these pigs to do shit. She'll die before we get to her," Donte said, beating his fist into his hand.

I punched a hole into my wooden cabinet and held my breath, screaming inside. I was so pissed off.

Finally, lowering my head, I said, "I will not let her, or anyone, hurt Reneece or my child. We will save them."

Donte walked closer to me. "We need a plan and a good one."

Agreeing, I said, "I know. But she can't know you're there because if she does, it's a wrap."

"E, man, that's my sister. Not only are you my bro-in-law, but you were also my brother and best friend before you even got with my sister. I got yo' back," Donte reminded me.

I crossed my arms and tapped my fingertips on my elbows. "We gotta find a way to ditch 5-0 and get her out safe and sound. The detective said they were here to keep me safe. But they focused on the wrong thing."

The detective interrupted our brotherly moment, letting us know he and one other cop would remain. The others were leaving. When they left, we made our way back to living room area.

We stood in the living room watching some officers depart my apartment and whispered, trying to devise a plan. Outside of killing Dareen, our biggest mission was to ensure Reneece got out unharmed and alive. During our conversation, someone started banging on the door. When Donte answered, it was Jalisa. She was barely able to stand, and blood poured through her pants leg.

She was trying to suppress the bleeding before passing out and said she had something important to tell us, but she couldn't get the words out before her eyes closed. It was probably from the loss of blood. Running toward my front step, Elizabeth, Reneece's other line sister, appeared.

Elizabeth was pressing her hands on Jalisa's wounds. "I tried to get her to a hospital, but she wanted to come here. She said some girl named Dareen showed up, using her as a pawn to get Reneece. She remembered dragging Reneece out of her apartment but had no clue where they went."

"How did you get to her?" Donte asked.

"She managed to call me since I live up the street. I came over right away and found her on the floor."

Detective Peterson came to the door. He helped with controlling the bleeding, while the other officer reached out to a paramedic. Not even five minutes later, an ambulance arrived to take Jalisa to the hospital.

As they put Jalisa in the back, Elizabeth, Donte, and I stood outside talking briefly.

Elizabeth crossed her arms and went off. "Whatever y'all planning, I want in. That bitch fucked with the wrong ones."

Looking at the two of them, I told her, "Nah, sis, you stay with Lisa. Me and Donte got this."

Elizabeth said nothing. Donte took her hand and said, "Trust me, she will get everything she deserves."

Elizabeth looked at us and finally nodded. So she got into the ambulance with Jalisa. We pretended to follow behind them so the police wouldn't follow us. It was the only way to keep them out of it.

When we realized we weren't being followed, we pulled over to MLK Blvd. to get our plan together. I texted Reneece's phone to let Dareen know I was alone as promised and heading that way.

"I'll wait for the signal," Donte said. "I won't risk my sister's life like that if she just wants you to show up."

Looking over at him sitting on my right, I said, "Yeah, I'll shoot once in the air, then, bro, come in and get Reneece to safety if I can't get out."

Donte was rolling up a blunt as we got closer. "And if you can't handle what's happening, I'll be right in. The only one dying tonight is that ho."

Donte dapped up Eric before they drove to the address that was provided.

Thirty minutes later, we pulled up to an old, empty building in the middle of nowhere in Durham. He pointed out Reneece's car parked on the side, near an exit to the building.

Being cautious, just in case they were in her car, I had Donte duck down in the backseat. We pulled up and parked directly in front of her black Camry. No one seemed to be in there or responded to me flashing my headlights. Donte and I sat and waited for a sign, then my phone rang. Looking at the caller ID, I saw that it said *Private Caller*. I assumed it was them, and I was right.

I answered the phone. "Hello? Dareen?"

"Come to the side entrance. You're alone, right?" she questioned.

I answered, "Yeah, I'm alone. I'm coming now.'"

Hanging up the phone, I did as I was told. Donte and I were still keeping our plan in motion. He waited outside by my car as I crept to the side door of the warehouse.

I found Reneece sitting on the ground. A red bandanna was tied around her mouth, and huge tan ropes held her arms and legs. I couldn't take seeing her that way.

"Babe." Rushing toward her, sitting on the cold cement floor, I removed the bandanna from her mouth and then embraced her. I just needed to feel her touch. I was so thankful just to have her okay and alive.

I said, "I'm going to get you out of here."

Reneece was overjoyed to see me but at the same time, startled. "Eric, Eric!" She looked terrified.

"Babe, chill out. I'm almost done. You take my keys and leave. Don't look back; just go," I ordered.

"No, Eric . . . She's here," Reneece mentioned, her almond-shaped eyes filled with terror.

I examined her, looking at her wounds. "What?"

"We aren't alone. She's somewhere in here. We have to be careful. She can come in here at any moment. She may even be watching us right now," Reneece whispered.

As I was freeing Reneece from her bondage, I saw Dareen emerging from the shadows. I quickly tried to finish untying the ropes before Dareen could get any closer.

"Hey, Eric," Dareen said. "You're such an asshole. You could've avoided all of this, you know?"

"And you're a crazy, motherfucking bitch, who didn't have to go this damn far," I snapped back at her.

Turning her back and going up some stairs to an office, she ran her fingers across the rail. "I'm just in love. The first night you fucked me, I knew it was the beginning of something special."

Calmly, I stated, "I'm in love too, Dareen, and it's not with you. You need to understand that. This can all be over. Just let us go."

Banging her fist on the steel rail holding her up, she said, "No, you do love me. I *know* you do."

Looking up at her standing by the office, I said, "I never loved you. And I never will. Don't you get it? Whatever made you think that, get it out of your fucking head."

"No! No, you don't fucking mean that shit. Take it back. Take it back, now." She shot several times. It wasn't as if she was aiming for us. She was just shooting in the air. Finally, her clip ran empty. She went into a dark office, then came back, cocking her gun.

"Eric, you *will* love me. And *not* her," she shouted, running to us from the top of the warehouse's steel steps.

I created this monster, and I had to be the one to end it. I knew that one of us was going to die, or both of us would. I was so ashamed of myself. My thoughts raced about my child growing inside of my wife-to-be and the lives we could have had. Karma was hitting me way more than needed at this moment.

"Eric, Eric!" Reneece pulled me down to the floor with her. "What's wrong with you? We have to get out of here."

I whispered into her ear, "Your brother's outside. I want you to go when you have a chance. I'll distract her, and you leave."

Reneece grabbed my pants leg. "I'm not leaving without you. I can't live or do this without you."

"Baby, I promise everything will be okay," I assured her, knowing deep down inside I was scared of this lunatic.

Dareen stood there watching us interact. Her face began to wrinkle. Her eyes scrunched together closely, piercing through us. She would've burned a hole straight through us if she had had laser vision.

Dareen shouted as she cried out, "If I kill her, you'll have to love me. You'll have to be with me. Don't you see? Can't you see what you mean to me?"

She walked closer to us, aiming her gun directly at Reneece's head. Dareen was out of her mind, but I couldn't let her get any closer or pull the trigger. I knew she wouldn't hurt me, so I would be the sacrifice.

Jumping in front of Reneece, knowing if Dareen pulled that trigger, it would be me who would be shot, I told her, "She didn't hurt you. I did. Please just let her go. Keep me here; just let her go. I'll do whatever you want. Just please, let her go."

Dareen stopped in her tracks. "I do like when men beg. So, I can keep you if I let her go free and not harm her anymore?"

"Yes. Whatever you want. Just let her go." I smiled at Reneece as she shook her head. I grabbed her hand, trying to give her some peace.

"Okay," Dareen stepped in between us for a brief second. "I'll let her go. But you have to stay."

"No! That's not fair, damn it," Reneece shouted, pushing Dareen down. I pulled her into my arms.

I held Reneece tightly, giving her the most passionate kiss I could, in case it would be the last one.

Departing my lips from hers, I brushed my hand across her cheek, giving her a dashing smile. "Goodbye, my love. I will see you soon. Remember what I said. Now, *run,*" I instructed.

I watched Dareen pull her from my grasp. "Either you leave now, or you'll die right here," she said.

I whispered, *"I'll be fine,"* to Reneece as she let go of my hand and ran toward the exit on the side of the building.

Dareen waited until Reneece was close to the exit. Then she shot me in the leg and said, "Now, you're mine, bitch."

Chapter 17

Reneece & Dareen

I was almost out of the warehouse when I heard the shot go off. My heart sank to the pit of my stomach. I glanced and saw Eric shake his head at me. No matter how hard I wanted to return, I knew he was doing what was needed to save me. Using all my strength, I pushed open the heavy door, leading me to an open parking lot. At first, there was nothing, so I ran around the building, finding two cars and a man standing out front.

I bent down, grabbing a medium-sized rock as I approached the cars. Suddenly, I heard a familiar voice call out to me.

The man approached me. "Reneece? Reneece, is that you?"

"Donte?" I asked, running closer to the man.

Picking me up into his arms, he asked, "Little sis, are you OK? I gotta get you out of here."

Tearfully, I nodded, telling him, "We can't leave yet. Eric's still in there. We have to get him out first."

Stroking my hair, he said, "You need to be as far from here as possible. He has a plan. I'm sure he'll be okay."

Pushing him away, I said, "I'm *not* leaving without him. Do you hear me? I am *not* leaving this spot until he's away from her!"

Donte held my hands. "Sis, I promise I will take care of this." Grazing my face with his hand, he said, "Here. Eric gave me his extra key to your car. Go ahead now. I'll make sure he gets home. I promise."

I hesitated, knowing that my fiancé's life was at risk. I had confidence in my brother, but I had to do something myself. They had a plan, and I would have one too. I finally agreed to leave. I took the keys, got into the car, and pulled off, but I didn't go far. I drove down the street, turning off my lights. I gave myself five minutes before returning to the scene.

Dareen

After I let that homewrecker leave, it was just Eric and me. I was overjoyed knowing we could finally be together. The little flesh wound I gave him would heal quickly. I pulled his body from the ground into the folding chair nearby.

"Why couldn't you just leave us alone?" he asked while I bent down to tie his feet.

Placing my gun on the ground, I said, "This would've never happened if you would've chosen me. You still can. You saw I let her go. We are perfect for each other."

Eric rolled his eyes at me. "You knew I didn't want you. You were a mistake. I keep telling you that."

Pulling my army knife from my sock, I sliced his arm. "I was *not* a mistake! I was not a *fucking mistake!*"

Using his free hands, he snatched the knife from me. "Yes. Yes, you were. I never told you that we would be together or that I wanted to be with you. You know that."

I picked up my gun and aimed it at him. "You can give her a baby, but not me? You were going to leave me in the clinic. You were so happy I wasn't pregnant. But for her, you're so happy."

I kicked his feet because he was trying to get loose from the ropes.

"Dareen, yes, I was happy because we weren't meant to have anything but the time we did. Reneece, she's my fiancée. She's my life. I am way more ecstatic about our first baby than anything."

"*I'm* supposed to be your fiancée. This is about *us*," I shouted.

"There is no *us*," he shouted back, finally breaking free from the ropes and hopping out of the chair.

I was losing my shit. I picked up and threw everything in my path. I grabbed my gun from the ground. Eric backed up, thinking I was going to shoot him. I wanted to, but instead, I pulled the trigger three times into the ceiling. I didn't understand why he wouldn't just love me.

He tripped over the chair, falling to the ground as he tried to back away from me. His fresh pack of Newport 100s fell to the floor. Coming closer to him, I picked up the pack and beat it inside my palm.

Pulling out one of his cigs and placing it to my lips, I lit it and took my first hit. "Eric, we can make this simple if you can understand. See, if I can't have your ass, no one will. There's a way we can all walk out of this."

"There's no way I'm walking or doing anything with you. You have caused enough havoc in my life," he responded, crawling backward on the ground.

I grabbed one of the other folding chairs and pulled it between us. Taking another puff, I threw my head back, exhaling the smoke into the air. I was about to sit down when I heard the sound of footsteps coming from behind.

"I thought you came alone," I said to Eric.

"He was never alone," the deep, dark voice said behind me.

When I turned to see who it was, I saw a gun aimed at my chest. He shot me, and I fell to the ground. I felt my chest. Blood covered my fingertips.

"Eric, I love you," I whispered before resting my back against a plastic shelf on the floor.

Reneece

I had come back to the warehouse where Dareen held me captive to find Donte nowhere outside. I slowly entered the warehouse, parking my car behind Eric's. I'm sure they didn't hear me pull up or get out of the car. Before leaving my vehicle, I found the detective's card. I called him, but it went straight to voicemail, so I left him a message.

This is Reneece. Eric and I are in danger. Dareen kidnapped us, taking us to some abandoned warehouse. I will text you the address. Please hurry. She's trying to kill him.

I peeked my head into the side door I came out of and saw Eric and Donte facing off, and Dareen was against some table with her hand over her chest, and her eyes closed.

Donte was standing there looking at Eric. Eric looked relieved to see him there. And without knowing if she was dead or alive, he was ready to get the fuck out of that building. Eric hobbled near my brother, hoping he would help, but he was wrong.

He grabbed a pack of cigarettes from the ground. "Where's Reneece? Is she safe?"

Donte let out a chuckle. "Yeah, my sis is safe."

Eric was holding on to the beam in the middle of the floor for balance.

"Can you help me out? I don't think I can walk to the car by myself."

Moving back a tad from Eric, he said, "Ha-ha, you funny, my nigga. Nah, brah, I ain't helping you, but I'm gonna help my sis."

Eric was dumbfounded. "What? What are you saying?"

My brother began sniffling. "My moms wouldn't be in the hospital, my other sister is fucking dead, and Neece wouldn't have been in this mess if it wasn't for you."

Eric shook his head, then hung it low. "I had nothing to do with what Dareen did. I did everything in my power to prevent it, but I couldn't predict any of this. I didn't want this for her or any of you."

Donte screamed at Eric. "But you fucked her! Probably more than once. You ain't innocent in this shit, my nigga."

"And I made sure I proved myself to Reneece. I'm still proving myself daily to show her I'm worthy to be her man and husband and help her forgive me. I had nothing to do with that ho lying over there in months. Don't you believe me?" Eric questioned.

Donte placed the gun to his side. "Yeah, and she ends up being the fool again. I ain't letting nobody hurt my sister anymore."

Eric took a deep breath. "You overreacting. You buggin' out. You acting like I was still fucking this bitch."

As he reloaded his gun, he said, "Who fucking knows, my nigga? I can't see no ho acting like this if you weren't. Or maybe she was just plain crazy."

"So, what you gonna do? Huh? You all of a sudden switching up on me, nigga?"

Donte moved in closer. "Your child is going to be fatherless, and Reneece don't need you. She's better off without you. Look what you put her through—our whole family! You deserve all of this."

Eric shouted, "You going to kill me? We supposed to be bros."

My brother yelled at him, "You stopped being my bro when this bullshit happened. Fuck you."

Eric held his leg, hobbling over toward my brother. Donte had his gun loaded, cocked, and ready to fire. I was confused about what was going on. What Donte had planned didn't seem like the original plan he and Eric discussed.

"You got any last words?" Donte asked, pointing the barrel of the gun into his chest.

Standing there, Eric glanced over the room and noticed me. He winked his eye and said, "Reneece, I'm sorry, and I love you. Take care of our child."

"You talking like she can hear you. It's too late, my nigga." Then he fired his gun.

As soon as Donte fired three rounds into Eric, I came from the corner running toward them.

"No! *Noooo,*" I shouted, rushing closer to them.

"Sis? What are you doing? Fuck, you were supposed to be gone." He stood in the way, blocking me from Eric.

I punched him in the chest. "*This* was your way of saving him? You *killed* him. You killed him," I shouted.

Donte tried to grab me, but I fought him off.

"You, bastard," I yelled. "What the hell were you thinking? I fucking *hate* you! I hate you."

When I finally reached Eric, he put his bloody fingers over mine and pushed out a smile. He said, "I meant every word I just spoke. I love you, and you're going to be an awesome mom. Just tell my baby that I love them." Then my love's eyes closed, and he stopped responding to me.

I shouted repeatedly, "Come back to me," and my brother watched me break down. I was beside Eric when I heard the paramedics and police sirens approaching. As if losing my sister wasn't enough, there was Eric bleeding, blood soaking through everything I used to try to control the blood loss. It was at that moment I wished I knew how to save him. Even to just remove the bullets that were killing him. I didn't want our baby to grow up without their father.

"Reneece," my brother whispered.

"What?" I retorted, not even looking at him.

"I never wanted to hurt you. I just wanted to make this right. I'm so sorry," he wailed.

Turning my head, I saw the detective, his backup, and the paramedics rushing in. My brother backed away from us into the middle of the floor. His .22 was pointed at his head, his finger on the trigger.

"Donte, what are you doing?" I shouted, confused about what was going on.

"I love you, sis," he said with his eyes closed.

Pow!

"Donte, *no*," I shouted, but it was too late.

One shot went off straight into his cranium. My brother's body fell to the ground. His eyes opened, looking in our direction. The gun slid to the middle of the floor near his body.

As the paramedics attended Eric and Dareen, I went over to Donte's body. One of the officers took his pulse, shaking his head no. I screamed out in agony. I lay across his body, refusing to move. I wanted to stay with him but was asked to move when the coroner arrived.

Standing in the middle of the warehouse, the police continued to ask me questions I couldn't and didn't want to answer. They finally left me alone. I stood there, looking at nothing but trails of blood on the gray cement floor. My world was over.

Chapter 18

Reneece & Dareen

I sat in my rental car, popping one of my Percocets to help with the pain I was feeling from the surgery. While waiting in the car for my friend, I started reminiscing about the night I almost lost everything.

I was in the ambulance when I awoke from them resuscitating me. At one moment, I thought I was going to die. I woke up, asking them where I was and what happened to me. They both asked me to calm down and said we were almost at the hospital.

They were able to remove the bullet from my chest. It barely missed my heart. I was laid up in a hospital bed with no visitors or calls. It was like I never existed. As my recovery process was almost over, at least for me to be in the hospital, I took it upon myself to remove the IVs from my arms. I peeked out of my room and saw police in the hallway.

The nurse was coming back inside when I scurried back to the bed. I pretended to be asleep when she came to check my vitals. I grabbed her wrist, asking why the police were out front.

"They said they were here for you. That's all I know." Her voice shook, and I could tell she was nervous about what I might do.

"Listen, ma'am, I'm not going to hurt you. I want you to help me get out of here. My mother is dying, and if they are going to take me, I want to see her one last time." Now, granted, it was a lie, but I needed to find a way out. Plus, she looked like the type who would be all mushy like that.

Needless to say, the nurse was able to sneak me out of the hospital later that night, completely undetected. When I escaped, I went to find shelter and food. That's when I met Joe. Joe helped me get back on my feet, gave me a place to stay, and got me a car to ride around in.

While I was reminiscing and waiting for my meds to kick in, Reneece finally came out of the day care with her daughter. I got information on her, where she worked, and their daughter's day care. But Eric, I couldn't get anything on him. So, if he was alive, I knew she would lead me to him.

Reneece

I picked up our daughter, Hailey, from day care. It had been a long day, and I was ready to get home. I'm sure my husband was awaiting our arrival, but I had a few stops to make before we arrived. I stopped at a nearby BI-LO to grab a few things for dinner, plus I was running low on diapers.

As Hailey sat in the shopping cart, I bent over, grabbing some diapers, and a young lady in a dark gray hoodie, sweats, and shades approached the shopping cart, playing with her.

"She's beautiful, how old is she?" she asked.

"Oh, thank you. She's almost 6 months," I responded as I placed the box of diapers inside the cart.

Her eyes still focused on my daughter, the stranger asked, "What's her name?"

"Hailey." I grabbed the handle of the cart.

Smiling at both of us, she said, "Well, Hailey, you're a beautiful princess. Congrats, Mom, on a beautiful daughter."

I was starting to feel a little uncomfortable. "Thank you," I said. "Well, you have a good day. We have to get going."

"Oh yeah, sorry. You have a good day too. Nice to meet you as well," the lady said.

I just smiled and pushed my cart as fast as possible, leaving the woman standing there. I kept turning around every few steps to see if she was following us. I was at the register when I finally shook off the bad vibes I was feeling. I thought, *It's been months, and that girl still has me shook. I got to do better.*

I headed home. Hailey was in her car seat, turned up, bouncing to music in the backseat. My baby loves music, so I blasted our song, "Soulja Girl," as she bopped her head to the beat.

We arrived home about twenty minutes later. My husband was already parked in the driveway when I pulled up.

Opening the driver-side door, I said, "Babe, will you get the groceries out of the car for me?"

"Yeah," my husband replied as I took Hailey out of the car to walk into the house. I stood Hailey on the floor, and she walked toward her father, repeatedly saying, "Da, Da, Da."

"There's Daddy's princess," he said, kissing Hailey on the forehead, then placing the groceries on the kitchen counter.

Grabbing me from behind, he asked, "How was work?" and placed a small kiss on my neck.

I threw my bags on the cream-colored chaise. "It was pretty good. What about you?"

"It was cool. I even beat you guys home for once." He laughed out loud while still holding me.

I noticed I never took Hailey's diaper bag out of the car. Tapping my fingertips on the edge of the chair, I asked, "Can you get Hailey's bag from the car? I forgot to grab it. Please?"

Biting on my ear, he responded, "Only if you promise to be real naughty before we go to bed tonight. 'Cause you tapped out yesterday."

He grabbed my ass real tight. I jokingly smacked his arm and said, "Eric, stop it."

My baby survived it all. Eric had survived the shots from Donte. . . . Barely. He spent three-and-a-half weeks in the hospital, but he survived. His recovery process from his wounds was the easy part. Having to bury two family members was the worst. But we survived as true couples in love would.

I was about six months pregnant when we decided to get married at the courthouse. We would have the elaborate wedding I wanted when our money was right. I had gained a job as a vice principal at one of the local high schools in Raleigh while my man was out here with his own construction and interior decorating and design company. Life seemed to be now in full circle and perfect for us.

As for Dareen, we never saw her or heard any information about her after that night. No one knew if she had survived the shot Donte gave her. At this point in our lives, we couldn't care less. Even if she did survive, she seemed to be long gone and was no longer a part of our lives.

Dareen

Following their car for over thirty minutes was becoming tiresome. Instead of going straight home, she stopped at every other store before going to her final destination. I played my position well. I stayed about four cars behind her when we finally reached their neighborhood. But another car cut me off, so I slowly drove down the street, hoping I could find their home.

I knew Eric wouldn't recognize my car. I was driving a midnight blue Honda Civic with tinted windows. Another vehicle was in front of me, moving slowly. It was a silver Jeep Cherokee. It slowed down as it approached a beautiful red and white town house. I wondered whose home it belonged to when I looked out of my driver's window and saw Eric and his daughter playing in the yard. The other car stopped in front of me. Being nosy, I waited behind them to see who it was.

The driver rolled down their windows. "Hey, bro, let me park. I'm coming in."

"Aye, Jalisa. A'ight. I'll tell Neece not to get too comfortable then. Park behind her. We gonna be in for the night," Eric replied with his daughter in his arms.

Part of me was glad Jalisa made it. She was just an innocent casualty in my war for my love. Anyone who has ever been in love can understand where I was coming from. Watching Eric interact with his daughter turned me on. He seemed like he was missing something, though. Maybe he was thinking about me.

I know when he spotted my car, he probably wished it was me. I could feel the atmosphere telling me that my man missed me. I plan to save him from this sham of a marriage he got into. But this time, I would have to be way smarter about it.

"Babe survived too. They won't be together for long. Eric, I'm coming for you, baby. See you soon," I whispered as I watched him go inside with his "family." But soon, he would know that I was here, and I was going to finish what I started.

To Be Continued . . .

Here's a Taste
of What's to Come.
Exclusive Preview of Part 2 . . .

Chapter 19

Dareen

I finally got home after a long day of snooping around, and I was tired. I made one stop before coming home. I had to see his face. Whenever I would catch him outside with his pretend family, he appeared so happy. I threw my keys on the wooden floor, which creaked with every footstep I made. Opening my refrigerator, I grabbed the bottle of Chardonnay Joe had given me a few weeks ago, then walked into my dining room area.

I turned on a little lamp in the corner that I stole from Walmart when I first got this place. I sat in an old, high-yellow rocking chair and stared at the wall to my right. Pictures of Eric and Reneece, their daughter, home, and their everyday lives were on that wall. They were taken over the past year, since the last time I saw them.

I sat there looking at them and talking to the pictures as I rocked back and forth. I looked at one of Eric's pictures, where he was standing outside his office having a conversation. Just looking at the picture turned me on. His beard was growing out, and his royal blue suit fit his body perfectly, especially the jacket. The way it gripped his swollen biceps, I could tell he had been working out.

Sliding off my purple tights and black thong, with my eyes locked on his picture, I said, "Eric, you know I'm here. I'm in love with you. We will be together. We'll be together sooner than you think. Look at how we survived. God has a plan for us."

I had a simple glass nightstand that I found outside by the dumpster. I took it home, cleaned it up, and now it sits beside my chair, holding my ashtray and the picture I drew of Eric and me. I turned to my left, where the table stood, and grabbed half of a blunt in the ashtray.

I didn't know if I was dreaming or if it was reality, but Eric was standing before me, waiting for me to come to him. Moments later, I closed my eyes and drifted off to dreamland. My dreams took me to the house where I first met Eric.

He took me into his arms, pressing me against his naked body. In a flash, my clothes were off, and I was bent over on a small twin bed, taking his dick from the back. As I dripped my juices all over his dick, he grunted, stroking deeper inside of me.

As I was dreaming, my body reacted to it simultaneously. My eyes closed so I could still see the vision of his thick, long, juicy caramel dick pumping my tight pussy. I spread my legs, one on the arm of my chair, the other placed on the wall, and slid four fingers inside of me, stroking my cookie to match the strokes I was feeling in my vision. I could hear myself moaning his name as I went deeper inside of me.

He was all I could see and think of. I plunged my fingers deeper inside of me, stroking them faster and harder until I reached my peak. My body jolted in intense euphoria at the thought of him pounding out my pussy. When I finally came, I opened my eyes. That nut was awesome, judging from the creamy juices over my fingers and the wet spot I made in the chair.

I lowered my legs back down, then stood to shower. As I walked to my bathroom, I sucked the cum off my fingers. I looked in the mirror at myself, my fingers in my mouth, my shirt hanging off of me, with one titty hanging out. I felt disgusted with myself.

I yelled at my reflection. "You stupid, little, nasty bitch! That's not going to make him ours any sooner."

Clawing at the mirror, I shouted, "Fuck you! I hate you. Maybe if you would've been smarter, he would be home by now."

My reflection started laughing at me. "Oh, so you hate yourself now? Good, you should."

I laughed at myself while taking my right fist and punching myself repeatedly in the head. I looked up at the mirror, and the laughter faded away.

Staring at myself, I said, "Bitch, this time, I'm going to make that bitch, Reneece, pay, and Eric will finally be all ours! Vengeance is mine."

My reflection turned its head all the way around. "*Yes,*" I exclaimed. "We need to kidnap their daughter. It'll show them we ain't playing no games. We can use Joe to help us."

I smiled back at myself. "Yeah, bitch. That'll fuckin' show them. Eric will see who she truly is and be ecstatic that I'm back."

I laughed with myself, still staring in the mirror. I know I'm not crazy, but other people would think so if they saw me. That's why I loved talking to *her*. She was my best friend. She gave me the best plans, never judged me, and has always been here for me. Plus, she was the only one who understood my love for Eric. I was about to take a shower when Joe came to my mind.

I told myself goodbye as I went back through my living room. I picked up the pillow and walked into my tiny bedroom. Then I lay across my queen bed, pulling the blanket I had made with Eric's and my picture on it over my naked body. I pulled the matching pillow with his face closer to my chest.

I lay there thinking of how I would have to plan this perfectly. I knew I would have to figure out their daily routines to get Eric and Reneece right where I wanted them. Maybe even getting in close with a friend of theirs would work. A male friend or colleague would be easier to manipulate, I thought.

I needed a new identity, a semi-new life. I couldn't make money and be around those people if they already knew who I was. There's no need to give it up too soon. I knew when the time was right, I could reveal myself and get the man I loved. It was time to start putting my game plan in motion.

To pull off an elaborate scheme, I needed to get a new ID, Social, and a little job to make my story sound as real as possible. I knew exactly who to call to get that type of documentation. My wonderful downstairs neighbor, Joe.

Joe was originally from Jamaica, Queens, but moved down South about two years ago. After getting out of the hospital, I hustled my way into the apartment I was in. My landlord and his wife were some freaks. When I found this place from a Craigslist ad, I met with them to see what my options were. I remember our first interaction perfectly. The wife sat across the table, looking me up and down in her orange sweater dress, biting her lip.

The landlord said to me, "Well, Miss Lady, it looks like my wife is pleased with you being a new tenant if—"

Squinting my eyes, I asked curiously, "If what?"

"I know you are trying to get on your feet, so here's our proposition to help you." He sat in front of me, and his wife stood from her seat and came between us. "Give me and my wife a threesome whenever we want. No ifs, ands, or buts, and you can live here for free. Just find a way to keep your lights and water on."

His wife ran her fingers across my thighs, then up to my breasts, fondling them softly. "What do you think, beautiful? I'll even make it a better deal."

"What can make it better?" I asked, feeling my pussy throb from her touches.

"I will take care of your first two months of utilities. Just tell me the amount, and I got you." She sat on my lap, placing her big, juicy lips on mine.

I agreed at that moment. I became their play toy, but I enjoyed it. His wife had the most beautiful breasts I had ever seen. Her 44-DDs tasted so good when I sucked on them. I had my first encounter with them that day I moved in. I made sure to give them a mind-blowing experience.

So, for the past year, I had free rent, and it was all thanks to my great nookie. Suddenly, my phone rang, breaking my thoughts. I looked for it, but couldn't find it. I got out of bed to search for it. After going all through my room, I decided to retrace my steps.

My phone was stuck in the creases of my golden chair. Unlocking it, I saw I had a missed call from Joe. A text from him read:

Joe: Sexy, hit me up. I know you're home. Don't make me come get you.

I was going to text him back, but I decided to call instead. The phone went to voicemail the first time. So I called him back again. That time, he answered after the first ring.

"Hello?" I said, hearing loud music in the background.

"Yo, what up, ma? Where you at right now?" he asked. I could tell he was moving around a lot.

"Why? What you got going on? I need something from you," I said, hoping this would be an easy yes.

"Now, baby girl, what is it you need from me, huh? You always want something for nothing." Joe laughed in my ear.

"What's funny, nigga?" I was puzzled. "How is anything I said funny?"

"You want my Jamaican dick, but not me. Always wanting something, but I get nothing." He continued to laugh. "What is you want from me this time?"

I breathed heavily into the phone. "Joe, if I let you hit this pussy, will you let me get two dimes of weed, a driver's license with a different name, and a Social?" I asked while I sat back in the chair.

"Your ass betta be suckin' and fuckin' this dick all night long for all the shit you asking for." He laughed at me again.

"You know if that's what you want, big daddy, I will. I'm tryin'a get a job, but they not going to let me if I give them my real shit. Plus, you have the best weed ever. A bitch need to blaze one." I tried to put my sexy voice on to make him give in.

He coughed into the phone. "If you don't flake on me, I'll take good care of you."

I leaned back on the chair and replied, "OK, Joe."

I could hear his lighter flicker. "Come on downstairs. I'll take good care of you like I just said."

"I'll see you in a few," I said, disconnecting the call.

Joe could get anyone anything. He had the right equipment to make the IDs and Socials, but he was working with someone until he got his shit to look legit. No one would question or think twice about the documents he provided me. They were that official. I had to take a shower to get myself together before seeing Joe. After my shower, I rubbed on the pillow one last time before leaving my apartment.

I kissed the pillow and said, "All of this, everything I'm doing, I'm doing for you—for us. You will soon see."

When I arrived at Joe's apartment, I found the door unlocked. He told me to just come on in and lock the door behind me. When I looked up, I saw him standing in the middle of his living room, naked. His dick was saluting me, his dreads were loose and down on his back, and his tattoos were very visible. It was how he worked out. He was like a caramel Jamaican god. He turned, giving me a slight smirk, showing off his pearly white teeth. Joe was about 32 years old. He was very mature, hardworking, and very sexual.

Looking at me all seductively, he said, "You going to get to work, or you just going to stand there and look at me?"

I slowly walked toward Joe, and when I got in front of him, I dropped to my knees, commencing the art of fellatio on his dick. Joe grabbed the back of my head and almost knocked off my wig as he moaned in pleasure. Before he allowed me to taste his nut, he decided that he was going to fuck me until I begged him to stop.

He pulled away and picked me up, sliding his dick inside of me. I screamed with pleasure as he plunged all ten inches inside of me, nice and rough. I loved it.

Then he threw me on the couch, deep stroking me. His beautiful caramel-brown skin was smooth, and his chest rippled like an African god. I couldn't help but admire his gorgeous body. When Joe felt himself coming, he slid out of me, forcing his dick down my throat. As I gagged on his rod, he moaned in ecstasy, saying, "You're my girl now." He came inside my mouth, filling it with his semen. Then he waited until I swallowed it all before removing his cock.

He began interrogating me as he went to the bathroom to wash himself. But Joe needed to know nothing about my business or what I had planned to do.

"So, what you need that stuff for?" he probed, walking back toward me.

"The weed is to smoke, and the rello is to put the weed into," I said sarcastically.

"You trying to be a smart-ass?" he said, chuckling, "No, the IDs and shit."

"Tryin'a get some work done, and till I get this rep off my record, I need new info to get some legit paper, you know?" I stated, lying back on his coffee-colored sofa.

"Well, you know," Joe said before inhaling the blunt, "just live here. You're mine. But if you fuck me over in any way, you will never see the light of day again."

Without realizing what I was agreeing to, I said OK. Joe passed me a blunt, then went to work.

He called up one of his homies, Pyrhoshawn, to order the driver's license and Social I needed. Then he let me continue smoking while he lowered himself to the floor.

"As my woman, you will let me do as I please," he said, spreading my legs. "Right now, I want to please you. So, you will take this tongue. If you run or burn me with the blunt, I will spank you."

"Yes, daddy," I responded.

Joe began to play and eat my pussy. I leaned my head back and enjoyed every minute of it. I wanted to be more attracted to him, especially after everything he had done for me, but when I looked down at his face, I could only envision Eric devouring me instead. Gyrating my hips on his tongue, I closed my eyes as my thoughts drifted off to Eric. In my mind, I thought, *It won't be long, and we'll be doing this for real. I love you, Eric.*

Chapter 20

Eric & Tommy

Two Months Later

Life has been so amazing this past year. My private business was picking up and with my best friend and line brother, Tommy. We're killing the game. It was February 12, 2017, and we were heading to meet with our newest clients. Patrick and his wife Rosetta just bought a building to open up a nightclub in the Raleigh area. They wanted the most elaborate club in the city. As the most prestigious interior design and construction company, this was our biggest project yet and would bring in some serious money.

We were out at the new location trying to think of the best ideas because the building needed a lot of work. The siding seemed to have been destroyed, the roof needed to be redone, and the flooring was barely good enough to walk on. We had our work cut out for us, but it would be worth it.

Arriving at the building around five that evening, we were prepared to go over our design plans and the construction needed. Tommy seemed giddier than usual. I was wondering what was making him that way.

We were reviewing one of the blueprints when Tommy looked up with a devilish smirk.

"What the hell, man?" I asked, leaning on the table.

He threw his head back, laughing. "Yo, E, man, yo, this girl. Man, she's *so* fine. And she's doing something to me. I think I may even be fallin' for her hard, dog."

Standing straight up, I observed his body language. "Nigga, you serious? You talking about this mystery girl you been fucking with the past few months?"

"Yeah, man, she's amazing," he said with a chuckle.

"Are you finally in love, my nigga?" I asked him, walking to the other side of the table closer to him.

Tommy laughed me off, trying to dodge my question. As we conversed, the owners of the new club came in.

"Pat, Rosetta," I said, greeting the owners. We all extended handshakes. Patrick looked around the club and said, "So, we would like to know if the club can be ready in about eight months."

"Possibly, depending on electrical and plumbing. If all those areas check out, and we don't have any setbacks with them, it is possible," Tommy stated as we walked through the club.

Rosetta stopped at what used to be the bar area. "I would like to make this the most popular nightclub in all of North Carolina, maybe the whole country."

"I can dig that." Tommy eyed everyone with a subtle laugh. "We definitely will make this the best job we have ever done."

"Great. With all the money we are paying you all, I'm way more than sure you will make us proud. Especially since your company came so highly recommended." Rosetta couldn't keep her eyes off of Tommy. Those eyes were screaming, "*Fuck me.*"

In unison, Tommy and I nodded. "Yes, ma'am."

"Well then," Patrick said, looking at his wife, "I think we should let them get back to work."

"All right." Rosetta took her husband's hand. "Tommy, I have some decorating ideas I would like to go over with you one-on-one. Be expecting my call." With a wink, she turned around, clinging to her husband.

"Gentlemen, until next time." Patrick threw the deuces in the air at us.

"Yes, sir. We'll be in touch soon," I responded, looking across at Tommy.

"I'll walk them out." Tommy sprinted toward them to guide them out safely.

As he walked the owners to the door, I returned to analyzing the landscape and blueprints. When Tommy approached the table, I had a few ideas I thought we should go over.

"Eric, look at how the upstairs area looks now. What if we make the whole upper area the VIP space? Then, on another side of the upstairs floor, we can have a second stairway, maybe near the right side of the building. Make it a separate dance floor and bar and put some bathrooms upstairs," Tommy suggested as he explained his vision.

"And if time and space permits, maybe an elevator, or at least a service one. It'll help with transporting food and liquor up there too," I said, walking closer to the middle of the floor.

Tommy followed behind me. "Yeah, man, I think that shit would be dope."

"We got a lot of work cut out for us then." I was laughing while rolling up one of the blueprints. "So, in the morning, you wanna start getting estimates from technicians, electricians, and plumbers?" I asked, placing the blueprints under my arms.

Tommy picked up his sketches. "Yeah, I can start making a few calls now before it gets too late. We can try to get them here sometime tomorrow, have them look at the place, and go from there."

"Bet." I gave him a brotherly hug before departing.

Before I could head out, Tommy stopped me. "E, man, hold up. Let's go grab a drink. Shit, I need to tell you about Monica and I last night."

Nodding, I said, "A'ight. Well, let me call wifey first. I need to check in and make sure she and baby girl are okay. If everything's good, I'll go."

"Let's go to the Ale House on Hwy 51. You know they be pretty chill during the week," Tommy said as he walked ahead of me.

"That's cool. If I can't make it, I'll call or text you," I responded.

Tommy nodded while picking up his phone to make a call. Then he rushed out the door like he had somewhere important to be.

When I made it outside, he was pulling out of the parking lot. I threw my blueprints on the backseat of my brand-new 2017 navy blue Lexus. I couldn't get into the car fast enough when my ringtone, "One Love" by Trey Songz, came on. I set that ringtone for wifey because that's exactly how I felt about her and us.

"Hey, big daddy," she said sexually when I answered the phone.

I couldn't help but smile when I heard her voice. "Hey, sexy."

It sounded like she was eating with all her smacking in my ear. "How was the meeting? And how's the building looking?"

"It was cool. They want it done a little sooner than I thought. Girl, what are you eating? Is it good?" I asked, laughing about her loud smacking of the mouth.

Laughing out loud, she said, "My bad, babe. These fries are as good as fuck. But how soon are we talking?"

Chuckling at her, I said, "You and your fries. They aim to have it done eight months from now. They're a little demanding, but I think I can handle it."

Reneece sniggered. "Well, babe, y'all can do it. Even if me and baby girl need to swing a sledgehammer or two."

"You always got my back," I responded, grinning at the thought of her in a hard hat.

"You know it, baby. That's why you married me," she gloated.

We continued talking about each other's day as I got on the expressway to head home.

Suddenly, she asked, "Where are you? Are you and Tommy going out tonight?"

I hesitated 'cause I didn't know if it was a trick question, "Well, he wants to have some bro talk after work. I didn't agree. I wanted to talk to you first."

She sucked her teeth like she was getting a piece of chicken out of it. "Babe, it's cool. Go have fun. I appreciate you wanting to talk to me about it first, but I trust you. I'll see you when you get home. Are you going to eat while you're out?"

My mind went left when she asked me about eating, "Well, nah. I got a taste for my beautiful wife, and they don't make them like her anywhere. I have to come home for that."

"No, silly, food," she said with a giggle.

With a chortle, I said, "I ain't sure. If I do, I'll let you know."

"All right, babe. Be safe and have fun, OK? I'll see you when you get home." She blew a kiss on the phone.

Reciprocating the kiss, I said, "See you very soon. I gotta have those juicy lips on me for real. I love you."

"I love you too, big daddy." Then she disconnected the call.

I changed direction toward Durham to meet Tommy.

Tommy

I was sitting at the bar; the Ale House had a decent crowd. I forgot there was a Carolina and Duke game tonight. Since the bar sat almost between the two, the dark blue and Carolina blue colors were everywhere, which was crazy. I had just ordered some wings when Eric came and sat beside me.

"Man, it took you forever. I thought you went home," I stated, waving at one of the bartenders.

"Nah, but you know I gotta check on my girls before I do anything. I'm usually home." Eric placed his suit jacket on the back of the chair before sitting down.

"Fa sho'. Man, hopefully, if this chick acts right, maybe me and her will be like you and Reneece." I cackled as the bartender finally came over.

"So, tell me about this girl . . . Monica, right?" Eric said before ordering a chicken Caesar salad and a shot of Crown Royal.

While we waited for Eric's salad to come, I took a big gulp of my pineapple Cîroc,

"So, peep this shit, man. Shawty *wild*."

Eric guffawed. "Word? It's like that, my dude?"

I placed my hands on my head and replied, "Yeah, man. Monica is one hell of a girl. Very secretive about certain things." I lifted my head, tossing it back, reminiscing about last night, "But when I get her in my bed or her bed—man."

Eric shook his head with a chuckle.

"Sounds like you into her a lot."

"Man, in more ways than one, you feel me? Last night, I took her out to Ruth's Chris Steak House." I took a bite out of my fries.

Eric cocked his head. "She broke you, huh?"

"Nah, man, she treated me. Then she took me to her room, man." I was stuffing my face in between, but the more I thought about her, the more my big man got excited.

"Her room? She ain't got no crib? How old is she?" he questioned, looking at me with his eyes crossed.

"Nah, she just staying there till her place is ready. Shit, the way things are going, I may tell her to just move in with me; fuck her lease." I looked up at the screen to see the score as the Carolina fans cheered loudly around us.

The two of us laughed, toasted our drinks, and continued eating and enjoying the brotherly company.

"Yo, man, look. I never had some pussy like hers," I exclaimed, licking my lips.

"What?" Eric choked on his drink, trying not to laugh at me.

"Man, listen," I said, laughing along with Eric, "she can suck the skin off yo' dick. It's the best head ever. Then the way she sucked the tip of my shit. Man, make a nigga fall in love."

"A'ight, now, nigga, don't fall in love with the head or your dick, my brother," Eric advised as he sipped his drink.

"Shit, it's her pussy too. Her pussy so fucking tight and wet. She gonna make me give her babies ASAP, you hear me?" My dick was hard as fuck as I reminisced on how good her sex was.

Eric damn near choked as I ranted on and on about his and Monica's sexual escapades. We were chatting it up so much that we lost track of time. Finally, when Eric checked his phone, I noticed it was a little after nine, and he was about ready to go home, I could tell.

"When we gonna meet her? Shit, since you doing all this talking 'bout kids and shit. This must be serious, and if it is, I think as a family, we should meet her soon," Eric declared, making it clear that he wanted to meet her finally.

"I'll bring it up to her. But she's really nervous and funny 'bout shit like that," I replied.

Eric looked at me suspiciously. "Well, maybe she can hang out with Reneece for a little while and gain a new friend, especially since she just moved out here."

"Yeah, maybe her and Reneece can hang out, and maybe we can do some type of double date shit," I suggested, finishing up my last shot.

"Well, we'll see what wifey says." Eric grabbed his jacket, then dapped me up. "A'ight, man, get home safely. I'm out." Then he turned around to leave the bar.

I was getting ready to dip out myself. I passed the waitress a fifty-dollar tip when my phone rang. It was Monica. I was so excited for her Facetime because I wanted to show Eric who she was, but he was already one foot out the door before I could catch his attention. S I answered her call.

"Hey, beautiful," I smiled into the camera as I walked out behind him.

Chapter 21

Dareen

"This nigga Tommy is completely obsessed with me. My plan is working perfectly," I said to myself as I walked into my apartment. See, he had no clue who I truly was. I was just Monica Griffith, a girl from a small town in Georgia who moved to Raleigh for work after graduating college. I hadn't talked to Tommy in two days since we had some banging sex at the Hilton in downtown Raleigh. So, I figured I would finally call. I called once, and it went straight to voicemail. He called me first when I was getting ready to call him back.

"Hey, you." He sounded super excited when I answered.

"Tommy, why didn't you call me earlier?" I questioned as I threw my bag on the floor near the pile of dirty clothes.

Trying to talk smoothly, he said, "Oh, beautiful, I didn't see your call till just now. Don't be mad."

Giving him a straight attitude, I replied, "Whatever, boy."

"You miss big daddy, baby? Don't be like that. I know it's been a few days. I just been busy. You wanna see me later?" he asked, but I wasn't paying any attention to his question when I caught a male voice in the background trying to gain his attention. I hoped it was Eric. It's been so long since I heard even a whisper from him.

See, I met Tommy a few months ago while looking for Eric's office building. I was able to find out about his business on a Google ad. It even gave me the location of his office. So, that same day, I went on a mission. I jotted the address on paper and headed out the door.

I was parked a few blocks away from the office in a rental car. Tommy knocked on my window as I was just sitting, surveilling the area. I rolled down my window slowly. I was hoping he wasn't a cop. "Hello?" I said in a whisper.

"Hey, miss. You all right over here? You been sitting here since I went to lunch almost an hour ago. You lost, or is your car not working or something?" he probed, leaning on the car door.

Man, he was one sexy piece of meat. He reminded me of Dwight Howard. He was tall with broad shoulders and deep milk chocolate skin, and how his muscles hugged his dress shirt made him irresistible.

I told him I was looking for Eric's office for my boss so she could meet with him the following day. That's when he gave me just enough information for the moment. He lifted his weight from the car, pointing to a small brick building on the corner.

I couldn't go that day, especially since I had no real plan ready yet, so I played off the situation, telling Tommy I had to wait on my boss. He didn't press the issue; he just continued talking to me. He even tried to spit some game at me. I thought that man was super sexy. The way he wore his pants, I figured his dick had to be a decent size. Watching his lips move, I thought about how he would eat and fuck me. But I had to think long term. What could Tommy do for me? Once I realized the asset he would be to my plan, I quickly gave him my number, and the rest was history.

I was about to shower when I saw that Joe had called me a few times. I guess he saw the rental parked out front that he got me. He was becoming a pest, acting like I was his woman or like I owed him anything. And he always questioned my whereabouts, which wasn't cool to me. Tommy and I stayed on the phone, and he was starting to make me irritable, so I texted Joe, letting him know I would stop by.

Soon, I went downstairs to see Joe. I need a little something to help get my mood right. Juggling two niggas while strategizing a master plan to get my man back was a lot on me. When I reached his door, I tried to get Tommy to hang up, but he was being petty, saying he wanted to make sure there weren't any other guys around.

I guess Joe was expecting me because the door was cracked. I walked in, closing the door behind me, but couldn't find him. After an extralong-ass five minutes, I finally got Tommy to hang up. It was just in the nick of time.

I had just hung up when I felt a hard hand hit my ass cheeks. I looked back, and there was Joe.

"Damn, nigga, you could've said something. Shit, you scared me," I bellowed, moving farther into the living room.

"This is *my* house; I don't have to announce myself. Why you being so jumpy? Fuck wrong with you?" he asked, coming closer to me.

"Joe, don't start. You always think I'm up to something," I hissed, trying to get him off my back.

"You mine, you hear me? You ever do anything wrong to me, you wind up dead," he threatened me, placing his big, strong hands around my neck.

"You're choking me! Stop it, babe." I scratched at his hands, trying to get him to loosen his grip.

"Yeah, you like it when I choke you. Bend over. Give me my pussy," he demanded, releasing me.

Something told me to be a little more careful with Joe than Tommy. Tommy was real square, but Joe was a straight-up Rastafarian shotta. I knew he played no games. I loved how he manhandled me; it always made my pussy wet.

He stood in front of me like a Jamaican god, undressing slowly. He motioned for me to lift my sweater dress. I moved my hands down slowly over the burgundy corduroy dress, lifting it up slowly, showing off my bare bottom, then my black satin bra till it was over my head and on the floor.

Joe released his third leg and, pushing me against the wall, rammed his long, thick dick inside me. He fucked me against the wall, slow and deep. I clawed his back and bit on his neck while suppressing my moans. Keeping his dick inside of me, he slowly carried me to the bedroom, bouncing me on his dick along the way.

I continued to moan in pleasure. Joe was giving me the business to the point where I was climaxing after every few strokes. He removed his raw dick from my pussy slowly, allowing me to taste my juices. I gobbled up his dick, sucking all ten and a half inches of it with no problem. I deep throated him. No gag reflex here. I continued tasting my juices off of him until he yanked it out of my mouth.

Flipping me on my side, he shoved his dick inside of me, pumping my body while holding my legs. I couldn't control myself. The head of his dick hit my G-spot with every stroke, and I screamed out his name.

Whispering to me in between breaths, he said, "You marry me and have my babies, yeah?"

I dodged his question. My mind was stuck on how good his dick felt inside of me.

"Fuck me, daddy. Fuck me just like that," I begged.

"Mmm, you make me come . . . You make me come, baby," he squealed. His body trembled as he released all of his kids inside of me.

Finally, he lay across the bed, catching his breath. I took the half blunt out of the ashtray and lit it up.

"Baby, that was so good." I ran my left hand through his dreads while hitting the blunt with the other.

"When you become mi wife, it'll be like that every night. I'm sure sooner or later, you'll be pregnant. We'll have our own family." He took the blunt from me. "I gotta get ready for work. You roll the other one." He went into the bathroom, leaving me to think about his statement.

Joe was clueless that he was just another pawn in my chess game. I didn't want no baby by him or any other man. Joe went to shower when I finally responded to Tommy's text from earlier.

Me: Hey, baby. I dozed off after work. Yeah, we can meet up. I'll let you know when I'm getting dressed.

Tommy: OK, sexy, see you soon. (wink eye emoji)

I was getting dressed when Joe reappeared in the bedroom, half dressed. He did security work for nightclubs, and it was almost time for him to head on out. I usually stayed in his apartment while he was gone, but when he saw me dressed, he started interrogating me like I was a prisoner, asking me where I was going and who I would be with. It was just way too much. He was blowing my high, so I decided to leave.

Once I got to the bedroom doorway, Joe grabbed me by the waist and snatched my phone. "Got you. Unlock the phone, Dareen."

I snatched my phone from his hands. "Give me my phone, Joe. That's some bitch-nigga shit you pulling right now."

"Where yuh go now?" he asked, following closely behind me.

"Out, Joe. I'm just going out, okay?" I crossed my arms. "Let's not do this tonight."

"Out where? Mi cum wid yuh, yeah?" He was super pressed, but for no reason.

"Joe, let me go! I don't want to stay at home all night." I pushed him away from me, trying to get to the door.

He slapped me across my face and shouted, "Yuh listen to mi, bitch. Mi tell yuh ass. You better be doing right by me, or I swear that ass is mine. Yuh hear mi?"

"Fuck you, Joe. You *don't* own me," I yelled back at him, throwing one of his Bob Marley pillows near his face.

"Yo, you my woman. I have the right to ask and know where the fuck you be disappearing to late at night and shit." He screamed at me, making me nervous.

"Joe, please." I tried walking away from him, but he stopped me.

"You fuckin' another nigga?" he questioned, grabbing me by the throat.

"Joe, you're being crazy," I shouted as he held me against the wall.

"Be fuckin' another nigga, and I find out, you'll see what the hell crazy is then," he threatened. He was so infuriated with me for no reason.

Joe threw me to the floor and tossed my phone at my feet. Then he left me and continued to get dressed for work.

After that altercation with Joe, a bitch needed a good man around me. So I grabbed my things and left him there to stew in his jealousy. Yeah, he may have been right about me fucking around. But in all honesty, I didn't belong to either of them. Joe and Tommy were just my playthings because I only belonged to Eric.

I would see how the night went before I got another room. I returned to my apartment to freshen up a little and get dressed. Tommy was meeting me at the Marriott. That way, he wouldn't see this crappy place compared to his apartment.

I waited twenty minutes for Tommy to arrive. I was sitting at the bar in the lobby when he shot me a text telling me he was pulling up. I saw him appear at the main entrance. I thanked the waitress for the water and began to walk to the entrance. When he saw me getting close to him, he was smiling extra hard.

"Well, hello, beautiful. You look amazing as always." He reached his arms out for a hug.

"Hi, Tommy." I embraced his hug, feeling his hands travel to my ass, grabbing it gently.

He looked me up and down, admiring my physique in the medium-length purple cocktail dress I wore. Guiding me out of the hotel to the parking garage, he said, "I thought before you try to kill me with that pussy, why don't we go eat and grab a drink?" he joked, escorting me back to his shiny all-black 2017 Land Rover.

I laughed at him with a slight squint to my eyes. We went to Bloomsbury Bistro to have a nice, quiet dinner. Tommy treated me like a queen whenever we were together. It sucked that this would all end soon, but I knew Eric would do much better.

Tommy waited for me to sit in the chair. As I sat down, he said, "Monica?"

"Yes, handsome?"

He pushed my chair in before sitting down. "Can we have a different type of date night?" He scooted his chair up against mine.

"What kind of night did you have in mind?" I said, slowly rubbing my leg up against his.

"I wanna get to know more about you. Maybe we can be more than what we are now. I'm digging you, but I want you to let me in a little more." Tommy was cutting his steak but keeping his eyes focused on me.

"Like a relationship?" I struggled to swallow my wine.

"Yeah, I was thinking that we can be so much more. Maybe even marriage." His eyes twinkled with excitement.

I wasn't with that whole relationship vibe, let alone marriage. I just wanted to use Joe and Tommy until things with me and Eric were better. The timing was all off, and I knew this nigga was really in his feelings with me. I told Joe what I wanted and needed him to know. Some of it was fabricated, of course, but still, it made him believe me.

He tapped on the table, redirecting my focus. "Monica, babe, you heard me?"

I shook my head. "Let's take it a day at a time and just go with the flow of things."

"Really? We already been doing that. How much slower can we take it?" The frustration and disappointment were evident in his tone.

Exhaling noisily, I replied, "Yes, I get your point, and I'm not saying no, but I'm not ready to open up just yet or be around a bunch of your family and friends, you know?"

Tommy looked disappointed with my answer. I hated seeing him look that way. Part of me was starting to care about him just a tad, which wasn't part of my plan. I was hoping that would be the last of that conversation, at least till I was ready to see Eric again. I didn't want him to learn about Eric and me right away. This had to be handled delicately.

After dinner, we walked back to his car. He wouldn't talk to me or hold my hand. When we got into the parking garage, I decided to make a move to show him I was with him. I had to keep him on my side.

When we got into the elevator, before pressing level three, I aggressively pushed him up against the back of the elevator. I pulled his black blazer, pressing his body to mine.

"Kiss me," I whispered, my right hand moving down to his groin.

"Go 'head, Monica. I just wanna drop you off and go home. I'm tired." He turned his head trying to play hard to get.

"Babe, just one kiss?" I grabbed his dick through his blue jeans. He was getting harder with every touch.

"Whatever." Tommy then pecked my cheek. But that didn't satisfy me. By this time, I was really horny and needed something to pounce on.

"You mad at me, baby?" Releasing my hold from his cock, I grabbed his face, putting his soft, juicy lips to mine. I kissed him passionately, sticking my tongue wildly in his mouth.

"All right, all right, you win," he moaned.

"You gonna stay with me?" I pleaded, kissing him on his neck.

"Yes, baby, I'm gonna stay with you. But this time, you coming to my house."

Tommy hit level three. "Let's go home, sexy so that I can tear you up all night." His dick was pressed up against my ass.

With that, we left to go to his house for a fun-filled night.

Chapter 22

Joe & Jalisa

I watched Dareen leave my apartment, but I didn't chase after her. I knew something wasn't right. I told her enough about me, everything that was hidden in my past. I was a troubled dude with a lot of issues. When I was 34, I was locked up for attempted murder but beat the charge. That's where Dareen and I found our common ground. She told me they tried to pin an accidental murder on her. She told me she never went to court or jail for it.

I wanted to love and protect her, but she wasn't trying to let me, and it bothered me. Frustrated, I left my apartment and headed to Chapel Hill to work as a club security guard. Most nights, I worked at the same place, but I ended up at a new spot every now and then.

Tonight, I was at my usual spot, Players. It was located right on Franklin Street. Most of the students from UNC would come and were regulars. I arrived at the club around nine. I escorted bartenders and promoters in with the rest of the security. We prepped the top door and got our game plan for who would work at what station and who would be near the money station.

It was around eleven when my night became more interesting. These two ladies walked into the line, and the brown-skinned queen in her tight red dress and gold heels caught my eye.

With everything going on, the eye candy was good for my soul. I couldn't wait to get a real glimpse of her. They finally made it to the top of the line after ten minutes. I tried not to make much eye contact and remain professional.

"IDs, please," I asked them, holding out my flashlight. "It's five to get in, ladies," I told them as they dug into their purses.

"Reneece, ain't he fine. And he has an accent. I'm Jalisa," she said, handing Joe her driver's license. "Where you from, mister?"

"Jamaica originally, then New York, now Durham." I handed her back her ID, then searched her for weapons.

"I've heard a lot about you Jamaican men. I watched *Shottas*," Jalisa said, laughing hysterically. Her friend stood behind her, shaking her head in embarrassment.

"Can you stop acting crazy so we can go in?" Reneece asked Jalisa jokingly as she handed me her ID.

I gave the ladies their wristbands before moving to the side so they could gain access to the club. Her friend walked up the stairs first, and then Jalisa brushed me softly against my waist with her hip.

I watched her walk up the steps, trying to keep my thoughts to myself. I wondered where Dareen was, so after letting the ladies go inside, I tried calling her. I called her ten times, and she ignored every one of them. I wanted to leave work, but I needed to work until I got my re-up. So, instead of calling again, I sent her a text that read:

Yo' ass better be home when I get there. I ain't playing with you, Dareen. You make it hard for a nigga to trust you when all he tryin'a do is do right by you.

I knew that ho was hiding something from me. I even knew about her little friend Tommy. I didn't understand why she had to go somewhere else for what she didn't want from me.

The way that little cutie was eyeing me in the club made me wonder what her pussy felt like. The way her ass jiggled in her red dress had my mind going everywhere. Regardless of what Dareen was doing behind me, I had to remain faithful.

Jalisa

Players was jumping. The DJ was getting us turned up. Reneece was so busy as a wife that she just swayed back and forth until "Get Me Bodied" by Beyoncé came on. When we heard "Ladies on the floor, where my ladies on the floor?" she screamed, "Yeahhhh!" dragging me on the dance floor.

You would think we were still in undergrad the way we cut up on that floor. Then I wanted another drink, so we went back to the bar. The men in there were so scrumptious, but I couldn't get that sexy-ass security guard out of my mind.

It was about 1:30 in the morning, and we were stationed at the bar because Reneece didn't want to be on the dance floor when they played "O Let's Do It" by Waka Flocka. The timing was perfect. I was standing before her, turning up to the lyrics, when Joe headed into the club. He was making his rounds around the club, so when he headed our way, I made it my business to bump into him.

When I bumped him with my chest by accident, of course, I dropped my whole drink over him.

"I'm so sorry," I giggled, holding a napkin out with my hands.

"You good, Miss Lady." He stepped back, shaking some of the liquor I wasted from his hands.

"Mmm, I think you can make me do more than good. Let me formally introduce myself . . ." I set the empty cup on the bar, waving at the bartender to come my way. "I'm Jalisa, and you are?"

"My name is Joe," he responded, taking some napkins and trying to dab some of the alcohol off of his clothing.

"Joe . . ." I said in between my alcoholic hiccups. The bartender finally came, and I ordered another Holy Grail. Then I turned back, focusing on him. I reached for his waist. "Do you carry big guns?"

"Maybe, but I think that's something I'll keep to myself." He chuckled slightly with a quick glance at me before beginning to walk backward into the crowd.

"Can I see? You know, the big gun you carrying?" I reached to feel for his dick when he tapped my hand like a naughty child.

"I got a girl, so I'm good on that." He denied my advance, but I wasn't giving up.

"You do?" I asked, batting my eyes at him seductively.

"Yeah, I got a girl, Miss Lady." He stood in front of me, looking really tense.

"Maybe I can be your girl tonight, and if you like, maybe every night." I leaned against the bar, sipping my drink.

"Have a good night." Joe tried to walk away from me, but I couldn't let him out of my sight that easily.

"Who's the lucky girl?" I grabbed his arm.

"Who?" He sounded like an owl as if he didn't know what I was asking him.

"Your girl. What's her name?" I leaned against the red velvet ropes.

"Dareen. Her name is Dareen," he uttered, sounding annoyed with the thought of her.

I was drunk, but not that damn drunk. I was hoping he said a different name. I indicated for him to follow me. I wanted to go somewhere a little less out in the open where we could really talk, well, maybe fuck.

So we went into the alley near the club. I wanted some answers to the burning questions in my mind.

"Did you say Dareen?" I raised my eyebrows, startled by the name. It brought back those memories from when we moved forward.

"Yeah, you know her?" he asked me, becoming defensive.

"I knew of a girl named Dareen. She tried to kill me and my best friend." I laughed, searching in my bag for a blunt.

"Maybe there's more than one Dareen in the world," he stated, gazing at me with those beautiful big brown eyes.

"Maybe," I said blowing out the smoke in his face.

I could see his dick bulging through his pants. It needed to be free, and I was going to give that beautiful cock its freedom. The more I stared at him, the more I was ready to attack him like a ravenous predator. I could tell he loved the way my ass looked in this tight-ass red strapless dress I wore.

I lifted my dress and pulled out a condom, but he wouldn't take it, so I put it back inside my purse. That nigga was trying to play hard to get, but I wasn't hearing it. I could tell he wasn't getting what he needed at home, and I was here to show him what dealing with a real woman could be like.

I took out the condom again and handed it to him. "Safe sex is the best sex." I bit my bottom lip, amazed at how thick and long his dick was as he pulled it out.

"You can handle all this dick?" He licked those luscious lips, smirking at me. Then he rubbed my clit, breathing heavily, "You want this?"

I pulled him closer to me. "Yeah. Give me that motherfuckin' Jamaican dick."

Joe pushed me against a dumpster. I jacked his dick, begging him to fuck me. I *wanted* that man. He closed the lid to the dumpster, yanked off my panties, and dropped them to the ground. Then he lifted me on top of it.

He spread my legs wide, kissing my inner thigh before opening my pussy to suckle on my clit. I grabbed his dreads as his tongue felt good on this pink pussy.

He lifted his head, roaring at me like a tiger. "You ready for this dick?"

"Yeah, fuck me," I shouted, waiting for him to give me what I was waiting for.

I placed my dress in my mouth, he put my legs around his neck, and my ass was dangling off the edge of the dumpster. The way he stroked was nothing like I felt before. He would roll his body, then pump me, shoving his juicy, fat dick inside of me deeper and deeper.

The way his dick curved, hitting all of my walls, had my pussy screaming with excitement. This was the wildest shit I had ever done, and I loved it.

"Does your girlfriend's pussy feel this fuckin' good?" I taunted as he rammed inside of me.

"Fuck, no," he moaned, still pumping inside of me.

He felt amazing, but I knew Reneece would be looking for me sooner or later. As good as it felt, I had to find a way to break the moment. His soft lips against my neck did not make it easy.

Before he could explode his sweet nut all inside of me, I pushed him away. "When you come for me, I want it all over my phat ass. You should come see me tonight when you get off," I suggested while rearranging my clothes.

"Here's my number," Joe said. "Call me about three. I should be finished up here. I ain't done with that ass." He tucked away his dragon, biting his bottom lip, staring at me.

"A'ight, daddy." I blew him a kiss and clapped my ass cheeks as a little teaser before walking away.

I hoped deep down he would come and finish what he started. Lawd, that man had some *serious* pipe game. I know he was feeling the chemistry just like I was. I sashayed my half-drunk ass back upstairs inside of Players. On my way up those steel steps, my legs were still quivering from our little quickie in the alley. I would snatch that man's soul if he decided to come over later.

Chapter 23

Jalisa & Reneece

Tonight was such a blast. I can't remember the last time I danced all night, especially with heels. Life was so different after the baby. Eric and Jalisa were awesome, always trying to give me breaks so I wouldn't be so stuck in the house full time. We finally left the club at about two thirty, and my dogs were barking.

We exited the club, and the security guard from earlier was stuck in a trance, watching Jalisa's every move. If he didn't want her before, he looked ready for her now. Since Jalisa drove, I was stuck standing in my five-inch heels for another thirty minutes so she could go talk to some old classmates from Central she saw. I decided to sit on this park bench on the street in front of this other club until she was done.

Finally walking back in my direction, she said, "You ready to go? Girl, I can't wait to get back to my car and take off these damn shoes. But I gotta be cute walking back."

I laughed out loud at her. "Always tryin'a be cute. Where the hell did you go earlier? Like I ain't notice you disappeared for like thirty minutes."

She stopped in front of me and did a twirl. "I was getting to know a new friend."

"Mm-hmm, so you say," I side-eyed her.

We finally made it back to the car. Before we got in, Jalisa coughed up all the details she learned about the cute security guard from Jamaica she couldn't get enough of.

"You drive, girl. I'm too drunk." She tossed me the keys and giggled.

When we got into the car, she looked at her phone and said, "Mr. Security has a little friend."

"A girlfriend?" I asked, backing up out of the parking space.

"Yeah, a girlfriend named . . ." Jalisa got quiet as she went through her purse.

I couldn't help but laugh at how she leaned back in her passenger seat. Her eyes were squinted real chinky like.

"The world is so fuckin' small," she said as she took a little bag of weed out of her purse and put some into her small bong.

I chuckled. "Is it now?"

"Yes, girl. How fucking . . ." She paused while trying to sit back up straight in the seat. "Shit . . . but yeah, girl, how fucking weird is it that his girlfriend's name is *Dareen?*"

I hit the brakes in the middle of the street. "Wait! What? Are you *sure?*"

"Yes, bitch. Just like that ho who tried to kill us last year. Why would anyone else have that name?" Jalisa laughed, not really thinking much about the name, but that shit put me on edge.

Pulling over in a cookout parking lot that was so crowded, I was lucky to find a parking spot. Once I parked, I snapped my neck toward her. "Now, what the hell did you just say? Say that shit again. Her name is Dareen?"

Lighting her bong, she took a long inhale and exhaled slowly. "Sis, chill, I'm sure it's . . . What's that word, a coincidence? Shit, it's just a name. Her name is Dareen. Don't think that much about it. You wanna hit this?"

She was trying to pass me the bong, but I pushed it back to her. "Did you see a picture of the girl?"

I could tell I asked the wrong question by how she looked at me. Rolling my eyes, I started the engine. "Never mind. I'm pretty sure you were busy."

"You know I was," she said, laughing slightly with her tongue hanging out of the side of her mouth.

"Maybe it's a coincidence." I exited from the fast-food spot parking lot and headed to my house.

The whole way back, my mind was everywhere. The thought of it being a coincidence didn't sit right with me. Something seemed off about all of that. We finally were coming close to putting last year behind us, and to think that this ho is somewhere lurking in the shadows and could possibly hurt any of us, especially our daughter—it just was fucking with me.

I finally got to my house around three a.m. Jalisa was knocked out with her head tossed back, snoring to the gods. I had to punch her in the arm just to get her to wake up.

"Ow, bitch. That shit hurts," she screamed, waking up out of her sleep.

"Wake yo' ass up. We at my house, and you gotta go home," I told her while getting my things from her car.

"I'm going to get me some more of that Jamaican dick," she hooted as we got out of the vehicle.

Exchanging hugs, I said, "Thanks for the night, girl. I so needed it. Aye, ho, don't let him turn you out," I murmured in her ear.

"He better hope I don't turn *him* out. I'm a beast, you hear me? I'll snatch his whole soul," Jalisa uttered. Then she got into the driver's seat of her car.

I requested that she call or text me so I knew she made it safely to her destination. Then I walked into the house, which was as quiet as a mouse. Hailey's bedtime music was still playing softly in the background. I crept up the stairs with my heels in my hand. I opened the door to the nursery, and my baby girl looked like an angel. She was the best blessing I ever received.

After that, I walked into the bedroom, tossing my heels on the middle of the floor before undressing where I stood.

Eric rolled over, his eyes still closed. "Hey, baby, did you have fun?"

"Yeah, it was cool, babe," I responded, stepping out of my panties.

"That's awesome. I'm glad you had fun, babe. I know you needed a girls' night." Eric seemed to be fully awake now, sitting up in the bed. "Are you about to take a shower?"

I leaned against the wall near the master bathroom door, running my middle finger down the middle of my chest, "Mmm-hmmm. Do you wanna join me?"

"You know I do." He got up from the bed, pulled down his boxers, and released his thick nine-inch dick.

I tittered, taking in the view of his juicy dick. "I guess someone besides you is happy I'm home."

Eric came up behind me, brushing his hard dick against my ass. "Mmm," he moaned while kissing my neck. "I think he wanna show you how happy he is. But first, let's shower."

I knew he was trying to get us both off, but my head was still in the clouds. I wanted to tell him what I heard but didn't want to kill the mood.

I kissed the back of his neck and whispered, "Babe," between kisses.

"Yeah?" Eric turned around, pulling me close to him. "What's wrong? It's all over your face."

Resting my head on his left shoulder, I said, "Nothing. Just something Jalisa said that I can't get out of my mind."

Running his fingers through my hair, he asked, "What's that? What happened?"

I hesitated for a moment, still wrapped in his arms. Then I told him about the night.

"Well, she met this security guard at the club."

"And what does that have to do with this look on your face?" he asked, pushing back some.

"He told her he had a girlfriend named . . . Dareen," I uttered under my breath.

Eric's eyes grew big. He was just as shocked as me. "You sure? Maybe you misheard her."

I shook my head. "Nah, babe. She was adamant that was what he told her."

Eric rubbed my shoulders and said, "The detectives said she was possibly dead. It's been a whole year, baby. I doubt she's alive or still around if she thinks about all the charges against her. But I will check it out. In the morning, I'll call the detective and see if he can verify her death or whereabouts."

"Eric," I stated, "maybe it was a coincidence."

"No, Neece. Listen, you and Hailey are my everything. I will protect both of you. So, I will find out everything, OK? I got to make sure the bitch is out of our lives for good."

"OK. OK, babe. I understand. I still hope and think it may be just a small world." I was confident in my husband and his ability to keep our family safe, but I was a little mad at myself for fucking up the vibe.

I stepped into the shower. "You getting in, babe?"

He came over to the edge of the tub. I bent over, letting the steamy hot water run against my ass. I opened my mouth wide, sliding his dick into it.

Eric waited for me to catch my breath, then pushed me back into the shower getting in behind me. Lifting my body against the shower wall, he lowered his body, shoving his tongue inside of my pussy.

The way he ate my pussy had me climbing the walls. He removed his head, kissing me, starting at my clit, then my belly button, working his way up. When he got to my tits, he sucked and bit on my nipples. He finally looked me in my eyes, tongue kissing me passionately.

Our breaths were heavy, and the water hit our bodies as we made out, making it sexier for me.

"I think she's ready for me. What you think?" he groaned while playing in my wetness.

I could barely speak before he pinned me against the wall, telling me to wrap my legs around him and hold on tight. Then he rammed his dick inside of me, slowly stroking to his own beat. I squeezed my legs tighter around him, pushing him in deeper. The thickness of his dick was tearing me up.

Finally, he let go of me, took my hand, and bent me over to touch the tub's edge. He bit my right ass cheek before spreading them apart.

"Oh shit," he said with a snort.

"What's wrong, babe?" I asked, jumping out of position.

There he was, halfway laid out in the tub. He was cracking up at himself.

"I almost busted my ass trying to eat yours." He laughed his ass off. "I'll turn the water off. Wait for me at the sink. We ain't done."

Following his instructions, I exited the shower and stood at the sink. He followed right behind me. He tossed me over his shoulder, then returned to the bedroom.

Lowering my body on the bed, he whispered softly, "I love you and will always protect you and Hailey."

"I know," I responded, gasping as he entered me from the front. We made love all night, and Dareen was no longer on my mind.

Jalisa

After Reneece went into the house, I called that sexy-ass man Joe, seeing if he wanted to come inside of me and play. I called him twice when I got home, and since I got no answer, I went ahead and showered. Usually, when I go out, I just pass out when I get home, but just in case that man calls me back, I want to be ready.

I wasn't in the shower for five minutes when my phone went off. If that was him, he had to wait till I finished getting my body right for him. No man wants to eat or fuck a bitch that smells like the club and is already sweaty.

Twenty-five minutes later, I emerged from the bathroom. When I got to my bedroom, my phone was on 10 percent, and Joe had called me six times. Before calling back, I cleared my throat to make sure I could put on the sexiest voice possible.

I called back, and he answered within a couple of rings, saying, "I thought you forgot about me."

"Oh, I could never forget about you. Unlike you, I don't have a man at home to come home to. When I called, I thought you were with your girlfriend," I hinted as I lay across my bed, air-drying in my towel.

"She's no longer with me or me with her. But I want to focus on *you*, Miss Lady. Do you have your own place? I want to come see you," he said as I heard many people in the background.

"Yeah, you can come see me, big daddy. I would love to have you inside of me. I meant have your company," I giggled a little. "Where are you, and what's all that commotion?" I questioned, listening hard to see where he was.

"I'm at IHOP. I haven't ordered yet. I was waiting to hear from you. What would you like to eat?"

I didn't want any food. His voice alone was making my body melt. But any woman knows if the man is trying to feed you, let him.

"Can you grab me two pancakes with their chicken and waffle combo and scrambled eggs and red potatoes? Or is that too much?" I felt like I was ordering the whole menu, and the nigga just met me.

"Nah, that's cool. Text me your address, and I'll be there when I get our food." I heard him make a slight twitter before disconnecting the phone.

It took almost an hour for him to get here. I was nearly asleep when he called, telling me he was outside. I ran to open the door, still in my towel. As I opened it, my thoughts went wild. He was standing there in his security outfit, looking so scrumptious. I was ready to have him tear up my ass. The food smelled good too, but I wasn't hungry yet.

I escorted him into my bedroom, where the TV was on, playing old episodes of *Martin*.

"You look even sexier in the natural light. Sometimes the club will have people looking different, ya know?" he said, setting the bag on the floor. "I thought if you like, we can smoke, then eat."

This was going to be a good night, I could already tell. He pulled out a big-ass bag of weed, and I could smell it without it being open. I knew it was some good shit.

"Hell yeah, I wanna hit that. Your weed man must be the truth. I may need his number." I sat on the bed, grabbing the rello from him to break it down.

"Nah, I grow my own product. I only have the best. My shit comes strictly from Jamacia. I have my ways of getting it here." Joe was focused on grinding up the weed with his fingers.

"I have a grinder if that helps. You don't have to use your hands." I leaned over him, tooting my ass in the air as I pulled my nightstand drawer open and grabbed my pink and silver grinder out for him.

"Thank you." He reached for the grinder, placing the rest of the weed inside of it.

He ground up the weed, then set the grinder on the nightstand. "I want to get a little more comfortable, if that's okay?"

"Yes, please get as comfortable as you like." I reached into the IHOP bag, grabbing some of his french fries from a box.

Joe started slowly stripping, his focus on me. First, his bulletproof vest fell to the floor. Then he lifted his shirt, revealing his perfect chest and eight-pack abs. My pussy was pulsating. I clenched my legs together, biting my lip, watching him strip for me.

"Put some music on," he requested, tossing his phone to the bed. "The code is 1208. Pick something sexy for us to listen to."

I went into his phone and saw his iTunes at the top. I scrolled through his music. I thought he would have a lot of reggae sounds, but he had a good mix of all different genres. I saw one of my favorite Jamie Foxx songs, "Slow," so I tapped on it. Joe moved his body to the beat as it played, dancing for me like a male stripper.

When he got closer to me, his pants were half unzipped. I took my hands, slowly moving them over his chest. His dreads were in a ponytail at first. He took his hair down, tossed his head back and forth, and gently shook it out. His hair stopped slightly past his shoulders, and the tips were dyed honey blond.

I pulled his pants down as the song switched to Floetry's "Say Yes." When I finished undressing him, his long, thick dick was all in my face. I wanted to taste it, but he moved away.

"Not yet, my queen. I want to see *you*. Take off the towel," he instructed, slowly jacking his dick and waiting for me to strip.

He lay on the bed as I stood up and slowly dropped the towel, revealing my thick body. His eyes glistened as he looked at me while rolling up the blunt. When the towel was on the floor, he patted my bed, motioning for me to lie beside him.

"You are a very, very beautiful woman," he said, touching my naked body.

"I'm sure you tell your girlfriend that too," I teased, tapping his hand.

"I'm done with her. She wasn't who I thought she was. And I'm sure she's way more complicated and a big liar." He flicked the lighter, sparking the blunt.

"When did that happen? All night you were talking about her until I threw this pussy on you," I asked, wondering what he thought this was or was going to be.

"I broke up with her a few days ago. I say I still have a girl to keep from attracting the wrong one. I want a real woman, a wife, a family. Then you came teasing me all night." He passed me the blunt and wrapped his left arm around my waist.

Something in me knew it wasn't the weed talking, and this man was serious. I never hooked up with a guy at a bar, and we talked like this. I lay there taking a hit and choked as I exhaled. This was some good shit. His hardened cock was pressed into my back. After I got all my coughs out, I turned my body around and sat on my knees.

I put the blunt in the ashtray and looked at Joe's hazel-brown eyes. "Show me how beautiful you think I am."

Joe pulled me on top of him, moved my head to the side, and sucked on my neck. "Put that punnani on my face."

Without any hesitation, I climbed to the head of the bed and sat my phat pussy on his face. I gripped my wooden headboard as his tongue traveled my pussy, and he stuck one of his fingers in my booty.

I began to talk dirty to him in between moans and screams. "Fuck yeah. Mmmm, daddy, eat this fuckin' pussy. Shit . . ."

He moaned as he sucked on my pearl. He stroked his finger in and out of my ass while he nibbled on my clit. I rose up for a moment, and he stuck his long tongue out, bouncing me up and down on it.

My 34-D cup breasts were hitting my chest the way he tossed me on his tongue. I've never been tongue fucked before, but it was everything the way he did it.

When he finally came up for air, I arched my back as he reached for a condom. "Come and get me, daddy."

Joe obliged and handled me the way I wanted. He stroked slowly and passionately inside of me, whispering how he wanted to fuck me raw and that he loved how my pussy felt. I threw my ass back on him, clapping my cheeks on him. I tossed my head back to see him. He had a look in his eyes like he was about to fuck up my life. And with the dick he was filling up my pussy with, I was going to let him.

"This my pussy now?" he asked while I still threw it back.

I didn't respond; I just kept going. Big mistake. He cupped my ass cheeks in his hands, tossed his head back, and threw my ass on his dick hard. I could barely take how hard he was banging me out.

"I *said,* is this my pussy?" he shouted over my moans, taking his dick out of my pussy and shoving it into my ass.

He fucked my ass while using his fingers to penetrate my pussy. He spanked me with his other hand pumping into me. My body wasn't used to no shit like this. I tried to run from the dick, but Joe wasn't playing that with me.

He grabbed my hair, pulling my head back, keeping me in place, "Don't run, baby. Come on my dick. Don't fight it; come for me."

I did just that. The brutal double penetration he was giving made me come like I never had before. I thought he was done with me when he lay down beside me, but he set me on top of his dick.

"Oh, you not done yet?" I asked, still trying to catch my breath.

Joe looked me in my eyes, mouthing the word *no*. I grabbed his dreads as I rode him slowly. He grunted, feeling my pussy grip his dick as I slowly moved back and forth. I wanted him to feel all of my walls.

I leaned forward. "If you are fuckin' with that bitch who tried to kill me and my bestie, I hope she tastes my pussy all over your tongue and dick."

He gave me a strong thrust. "Dareen is out of my life. I want you if you'll have me. And if she did what you just said, I'll never let her hurt you again. I'll kill her first."

He flipped me on my back, keeping his dick in place. I kissed the lion tattoo on his chest. "That's how you feel right now."

Tossing his dick into me slowly, he said, "No, you'll see."

He put my legs over his shoulders, pounding me hard, throwing his dick in a circle. I felt every inch of that man. It was the best sex I've ever had. I could tell he was ready to come as his stroke and pace sped up. I was trembling in ecstasy as I felt myself climaxing again. He let me get off my second nut before removing his condom and stuffing his dick into my mouth.

"Swallow my nut, baby. Take daddy's cum," he moaned while he felt my tongue flicker around his head. He pushed my hands away, having me suck his dick with no hands. When he was about to come, his body shook, and he let out a loud roar, stretching his arms out and puffing out his chest, releasing all his semen inside my mouth.

After making sure I swallowed every drop, he lay beside me.

We were cuddled up as I took my fingers, twirling his dreads around them. I said, "If you really did end it with her, I'll think about it if you show me you're worth my time and are different than these other dudes out here."

"You'll think about it? You're going to have my babies and be my wife." Joe grabbed me, kissing me softly. "I am ready to eat now."

We both laughed. "Yeah, I think we worked up an appetite. I'll warm up the food while you roll up another one."

With a quick bite on the back of my thigh, Joe said, "Yeah, if you let me be your man."

"Hmm, maybe." I left the room with the food.

As weird as it seemed, he gave me good vibes. And nothing he said appeared to be a joke, at least not to him, so I was willing to give him a chance. Plus, if he were fucking with the real Dareen, she would be getting a little of her well-deserved Karma.

Chapter 24

Eric

I couldn't believe what Reneece told me the other night. I feared for our safety, especially Hailey's. I couldn't live with myself if anything happened to her. I decided to go into the office late so I could try to dig out some information.

I arrived at the Durham Police Station around nine that morning. As I sat in the front waiting on Detective Peterson, my mind returned to the last time I was here. It was after they released me from the hospital. I was interrogated and not treated like the victim. It pissed me off. They finally let me out after sitting in a dark room for almost an hour. They never provided any information about what happened to Dareen. I assumed she didn't make it from the gunshot by Donte.

Finally, Detective Peterson came from the back. He greeted me warmly.

"Hey, Eric. How's the family? It's been what a month or so?" he asked, tapping me on the back.

"Yeah. It's been a minute. I have something I want to talk to you about," I said as we walked down the hallway.

"You hungry? Let's go to Blue Café. We can grab something to eat and talk there." He looked around him as he went into his office, grabbed his suit jacket, and then led me out the door.

We drove to the Blue Café, and I followed him. As I drove, I kept flashing back to the night I almost lost Reneece and my own life. On our wedding day, I vowed not to let anything happen to her again and would protect us at all costs.

I got to the restaurant, parking beside his black Chevy Impala, and walked in silently behind him. The waiter sat us near the bar. It was quiet, not much of a crowd. After ordering our drinks, I figured to get straight to the point.

"Well, hey, thanks for meeting with me. I appreciate you taking the time on short notice," I said, looking over the menu.

"Yeah, son, it definitely is not a problem. When you called and told me the situation, it sounded like a coincidence, but who knows? It is very strange, though." The detective looked at me, full of concern.

"Yeah, and my wife seems a little nervous and on edge. You know she worries, and I worry. If Dareen is still alive, and if she will come after us or our daughter . . . You have to understand." I closed my menu, looking around for someone to take our order.

"I understand. Eric, I will do some digging into the coroner's office. This is an unofficial investigation only until I get enough evidence to reopen it officially." He pushed his menu to the side and then started tapping his fingers on the table.

"Yeah, well, I guess . . ." I stopped in midsentence as one of the waitresses approached the table.

"Hey, I'm your waitress for today. I'm Naiesha. Are you all ready to order?" she asked us, giving me this seductive eye.

I flashed my wedding ring at her as I picked up the menu again. "I'll have the fried calamari with fries. We never got our drinks, so I'll take a gin and tonic on light ice."

"Okay, and I'll need your ID. Gotta make sure you're at least 21," she smirked. "And for you, sir?" She kept her eyes on me while waiting for the detective to answer.

"I'll just take the BLT on wheat bread if possible, no mayo, and a Sprite, please, with no ice." He picked up the menus, handing them to her.

"I'll be right back with your drinks, gentlemen." She walked away, swishing her small booty extra hard. I guess she wanted some extra attention.

"Look, I been working on this since you called me. I found something where we can start."

"Yeah? What's that?"

Detective Peterson pulled out a vanilla envelope. He slid it across the table to me. He nodded, giving me the okay to open it. Sometimes, when you go knocking at the devil's door, he'll answer, and that's what I was afraid would happen when I opened it.

Slowly tearing off the tape that sealed it, I pulled out the papers inside it. It contained official documents stating that Dareen's body was not found at the scene, in the morgue, or anywhere. She was nowhere to be found. It was as if she had disappeared or never existed. The report from the city had someone's signature I couldn't make out, stating she was deceased and that her body was cremated.

"So, she may be alive? No one knows? No one can tell us *anything?*" I got frustrated with the thought of our police being so unresourceful and unhelpful. No wonder serial killers get away for so long without being caught.

"That's possible. I'm going to the morgue and will dig a little deeper to see what I can find out." He took the papers back, placing them on the corner of the table as the waitress returned with our food.

Taking a bite of my calamari, I told him, "Yeah, find out. I don't want my wife or my little girl harmed by this bitch if she's alive. If you don't find out something, *I* will."

Detective Peterson looked over his food, then back at me. "Trust me, Eric. I'm going to get to the bottom of this."

We finished eating before he had to return to the office. After that, we left the restaurant. Before getting into his car, he shook my hand and gave me a fatherly hug.

I watched him back out before getting into my car. I wanted to wait and see what he could tell me before I made a move, but I wasn't satisfied. I found a private detective last night and decided I would give him a call to see if he could help my family, so I called him as I returned to my office to meet Tommy.

Detective Peterson

It was very curious how there was barely any information about Dareen's body or whereabouts. The paperwork was confusing. There was a signature from a Joseph Tarr regarding her cremation, but the other paperwork listed her and her body as missing. So, which of the papers was the truth? I planned to get to the bottom of it. And the sooner, the better.

After everything those kids had been through the past year, I wanted to be more involved with their lives. I had become their father away from home. It felt nice to be a part of their lives in a positive way, so I had to protect my children at all costs.

I arrived at the morgue and saw a man cleaning the hall with a name tag that read Joe. I wondered if he was the one who signed the paperwork and possibly hid the fugitive.

"Hey, good morning, sir." I approached the dark-skinned brother from the side.

"Hey, what's up?" he responded, mopping the floor.

I removed the toothpick from my mouth. "Do you know if Dr. Lorine is here?"

He looked up at me with curiosity. "Yeah, I saw her and some other doctors go that way."

He pointed down the hallway toward the elevators leading into the upper part of the hospital. "Cool, thank you."

"Yes, sir." He bowed his head, going back to work.

I walked past him, then doubled back to ask if he was who I was looking for.

"Hey, quick question. How long have you been working here?" I asked, standing close to the wall.

"About three years cleaning and stuff for a company. I work for different contractors, so I go where there's a job. But they like me here and vice versa, so I been hanging here." He pushed the mop to the side. "Why you asking?"

"No reason, my brother. But that's what's up. I like seeing my young Black men doing something other than running the streets. Continue doing your thing, young man." I reached out to give him a handshake.

"Word. I appreciate it." He took my hand, shaking aggressively.

"I'm Detective Peterson, by the way. It was nice to meet you." I let go of his hand.

"Joe Bachata," he replied, grabbing the mop handle.

"Is there another Joe who works here?" I asked, watching him move his mop to the middle of the floor.

He drained the mop before taking it out, "I think so. But I think he quit or got fired; not sure."

"Oh, all right. Well, thanks for chatting with me. Take care of yourself. It looks like the doc is coming this way. Stay blessed, young man." I nodded at him while turning my back.

"Yeah, you too," he replied as I walked away.

I hope I didn't intimidate him. I just wanted to make sure I wasn't missing out on any leads. Dr. Lorine came out of the hallway, and when she saw me, she seemed surprised.

"Doctor, nice to see you again." I flashed my badge to her as she came closer.

"Yes, Detective. Nice to see you. Is this official business?" she asked, walking past me.

"It's unofficial for now. Can we talk in your office?" I asked her, waiting for permission. I wanted to make this an easy visit.

"Sure, come on, this way." She walked ahead of me, taking me down a long corridor.

While walking behind her, I couldn't help but think about the last time I had seen her. I fucked her in the office on top of her desk. She wanted more, but being freshly divorced, I wasn't ready to make any commitments. She didn't like that, so things got messy, and I stayed away until last year.

We entered her office, and I sat in the black wooden chair and pulled the envelope from my jacket pocket.

Sliding it on the desk, I said, "It looks like someone created a document saying that a young lady named Dareen was cremated after she passed away. It also has two signatures."

She picked up the papers, put on her glasses, and looked at the documents. "I didn't sign this. That's not my signature. Who would sign this? I don't even have a copy of this."

"Joseph Tarr, who's that? His signature is there beside whoever that is," I questioned, leaning over and pointing at the document.

"He worked here at one time; he was my assistant. But I fired him a little over a year ago," Lorine said as she went toward the back of her desk.

"Why?" I asked, wondering if his firing and Dareen's missing paperwork had any connection.

Lorine folded her arms as she let out a slight giggle, then said, "Instead of working or doing something productive, I caught him with some girl on top of one of the tables where we got our patients out, and they were having sex. I was completely disgusted. I fired him on the spot and kicked them both out."

"The fuck?" I queried, raising my eyebrows.

"Yeah, nasty bastards," she exclaimed, standing up straight.

"Do you have any recent information on him? I need to reach him and find out what really happened to Dareen's body," I said, hoping I could get a decent lead.

"I'll look through my files; whatever I find I'll send over. As for Joe, I may have his current address." Lorine sat down at her desk, turning on her computer. "Most of the employees' information is in a computer database. I can see if any of his information is still in here," she informed me.

"Cool. When you find anything, call me or fax it over immediately, please."

I wrote my new phone and personal fax number on paper, then left her office. Hopefully, Lorine could provide me with some information.

Getting back into my car, I called Eric and told him where I stood with my morgue visit. Hopefully, he hasn't done anything irrational to find out about Dareen.

"Yo, I have a few minutes. What you got?" Eric said anxiously.

"Eric, I left the morgue. The guy who signed off on the paperwork was fired. I'm getting his address and all the paperwork they have on Dareen faxed over to my office. I'm about to head to my office. I have an official case to work on, but I'll get back to you as soon as possible."

"That's a bet. I'm finishing a meeting. Let me know, and I'll call you later." Eric was trying to rush me off the phone. I'm unsure if it was for work or if he was about to do something stupid.

"Will do. And, Eric, if you hear anything, call me first. Don't do anything crazy. We have no idea what she may be up to," I advised, hoping he would heed my words.

"I'm not, but I will be doing my own digging. If we both work on it, maybe we can get to her before she tries anything. I got to go. I'll touch basis later." Eric quickly disconnected the call.

After talking to him, I went back to my office. I had other cases I needed to work on. I would get more answers in time, but until then, I needed to keep my job going. I received a call from the chief stating he was giving me a new partner to train. I braced myself for a longer day than expected.

Chapter 25

Dareen & Joe

It had been a few weeks since I saw Joe, and I wasn't feeling it. He wouldn't let me into his apartment, and he wouldn't give me any dick. I didn't understand what was going on with him. Even with the voicemail he left me that night, I just thought nigga was in his feelings and paid it no mind. Maybe I should have. I needed him inside of me, and he was my connect.

I had no intention of telling Joe my plans until I knew it would work in my favor. Once I came back to Eric, he would forgive me for cheating on him with his best friend, Tommy, and Joe. I have forgiven him for carrying on his fake marriage with Reneece.

I was walking near my window when I noticed Joe's car pulling up. Going closer to the window, I noticed he wasn't alone when I went to crack my window to call his name. I hid behind my curtain to see if I could catch the woman with him.

Who the fuck is that? I asked myself. As I looked closer, I saw she resembled that bitch Jalisa. I knew I should've killed her when I had the chance. She was just like her friend, taking what didn't belong to them. I waited for them to go inside, and then I would confront them. They were all over each other, hugged up while Joe fumbled to get his key into the door.

I could hear them from the steps inside the building . . . her soft sounds of laughter in between groans. I knew what they were doing or about to do. I snuck down, seeing that they had forgotten to close the door completely, so I slowly pushed it open. I thought I would be caught sneaking in when the door creaked, but they were so intertwined with each other that they didn't notice it.

The two of them were tearing off each other's clothes in his bedroom when I sneaked in. I hid behind his brown recliner that was angled toward Joe's bedroom and watched as he delicately laid her body on his bed, kissing her entire body. Jalisa tossed her head back, almost knocked him in the face with her box braids as he ate her pussy on the edge of the bed.

Watching how he tasted her and hearing the sexually arousing sounds that got louder by the moment did nothing but turn me on. Watching them was like having my own personal porn hub. I couldn't help but play with myself. I tried to contain my emotions, but my pussy throbbed, aching to be satisfied.

Masturbating to the pace of his long strokes, I whispered to my pussy, "Don't worry. Eric will be back inside of us very soon. No more dealing with these crazy men. Daddy will be home soon."

Joe was reaching his climax, and it was time for me to hurry out before he was me. I ran out of his living room as he released his load on her ass. I could hear his loud, animalistic moan behind me while I ran back to my apartment.

I was so angry that he was fucking that cum bucket instead of giving me what I needed from him. He just didn't know his place, but he will soon discover that *no one* leaves me until I say they can.

Joe

I enjoyed every moment with Jalisa. Her conversation, the sex, her overall aura, it all made me want to be the best I could be for her. We lay in bed, finishing up a blunt before she had to get ready for work at the hospital.

"You're gonna make me kidnap you and never let you go," I said as I watched her get dressed, and all I could think about was taking off her clothes again.

She playfully hit me with her shirt and laughed. "No, you mean pussy-nap me."

"Do you have to leave now? You should stay a little longer. Come on, babe, please," I pleaded, hoping she would oblige and get back in bed with me.

"Joe, I still got to go to work, and so do you." Jalisa grabbed my dick while biting her lip. "I'll be back to you both before you know it."

"Yeah, I know. I'll be thinking and missing you all day." I held her waist, smelling her Strawberry Passion perfume that lingered on her clothes.

"But you'll see me tonight as soon as you get off." Jalisa gave me one last kiss before walking out the door.

It was hard letting her go. If I could have my way, she would be here all day, every day. I wanted to make all her dreams come true. I was going to shower when someone came banging on my door.

"Joe! Joe! Gotdamn it, open this fuckin' door, Joe," I heard the familiar voice scream through the thick wooden door.

"Who is it?" I yelled back, trying to put on my pants.

"Joe, open this mothafuckin' door right fuckin' now," I heard Dareen shout as she banged on the door.

I wasn't in the mood for any of her shenanigans, so I opened the door with a slight eye roll, wondering why she was even here. "What you want?"

Dareen flashed an impish smile at me. "I want you. Why else would I be here?"

"I'm good, man. If that's all you want, please leave."

Dareen pushed her boobs up in her black tank top, trying to get a reaction from me. "Joe, I'm sorry, baby," she said while running her fingertips across her glossy lips.

Sucking my teeth, I was about to let her know I wasn't a fool. "Dareen, I know you been fuckin' a nigga named Tommy who thinks your name is Monica these past few months. You thought I wouldn't find out or something? It hurt, but I moved on, so go do you."

"I can—" She was about to give me some lame-ass excuse, but I cut her off.

"Nah, save it. Whatever you got going on in that crazy-ass mind of yours, I want no part of. Have a good day." I turned my back, swinging the door behind me.

Dareen pushed her body in the way of the door. "You said you were my man. What happened to that?" She tried to seduce me with her voice, but it didn't faze me.

I turned back around. I didn't understand why she wouldn't just leave. "I ain't shit to you unless you want some weed. Actually, nah, find you another weed man. I'm good, shorty. We're finished." I was going to shut the door in her face, but she stopped me.

"Really? Is it truly like that?" Dareen ran her hand over my face as I turned away.

I tried keeping her from entering my place. Holding my stance with one hand on the doorknob, I told her, "Yeah, well, unless my child is in your womb, then we have no ties. And I mean that. Don't call or come to my house for shit. It's over, Dareen; let it go."

"You only doing this 'cause of the ho you fucking. I *saw* y'all. You ate her pussy, then you fucked her like you loved her. What type of fuck shit is that?" Dareen folded her arms, looking me up and down as if she were sickened by the sight of me.

"Yo, you stalking a nigga and shit? You really *are* fucking crazy." I whipped my hand over my face, shaking my head in disbelief at what I was hearing.

"I'm *not* crazy," Dareen yelled, trying to kick my door in.

"Yo, check yourself!" I shouted, pushing my index finger into her temple before she knocked my hand away.

With this crazed look in her eye, she said, "Don't call me crazy. I ain't fucking crazy, okay?"

I tried to push her out of my apartment. "Get the fuck out here, yo. Fuck out of my house!"

Reaching her arm toward me, she said, "Joe, you're *mine*, not that little ho Jalisa or whoever she is."

"No." I paused, confused about how she knew my girl's name. "How did you know her name?" She said nothing in response. She stood there with a stupid look on her face.

"Dareen, Monica, whoever the fuck you wanna be, I'm done, a'ight? Done. Get the fuck on," I screeched, hoping she understood what we had was over.

Before Dareen could back away from my door, she gagged twice and then threw up in front of my feet.

"What the hell, yo?" I yelled, looking at her, disgusted.

"I been like this for about a week. I don't know what's wrong with me, Joe." She tried coming closer to me, but I pushed her away.

"You pregnant?" I stepped back, eyeing her up and down.

"I don't know," she shouted at me, throwing her hands in the air.

"If you are, I want a DNA test before I do anything for you or that child." Then I slammed the door in her face. I had nothing else to say.

I couldn't care less about Dareen or whatever her game was. But an innocent child being involved? I had to get ready for work, but she fucked me up with that shit.

After talking to Dareen, I lay on my bed and debated telling Jalisa. But I always wanted to be honest with her. I grabbed my phone off the charger, scrolled to her contact information from my recent calls, and stared at it momentarily before hitting the call button. As the phone rang, my blood pressure rose. I hoped this wasn't going to be the end of us.

She answered the phone after two rings. "Hey, babe, I'm just 'bout to clock in. You okay?"

Clearing my throat, I said, "Umm, yeah. Dareen just came by. She tried to kick in my door. She watched us fucking and shit. Bitch is crazy."

"What the fuck? Yo, she sounds like the same crazy-ass broad from last year," she said, laughing slightly. "I hope she enjoyed the show. Next time, tell her we'll send her a video."

"She may be pregnant." My voice rattled as I got it out. I was so nervous to tell her because I didn't know what this would do to us.

"By you?" Her voice was a little shaken when she asked me.

"Possibly. I don't know. It could be this other dude, Tommy's baby," I muffled, not knowing what she would say.

"So, she was fucking around on you? Or were you fucking me and her at the same time?" she accused me with her attitude pouring through the receiver. "Look, if she is, and it's yours, we'll work it out. That was before us, so we can make this work. 'Cause I like you, so we'll talk later, OK, babe?" She let out a sigh as she paused, waiting for my response.

"All right. Have a great day, beautiful. Call me when you get a break, okay?" I loved hearing her voice. Hopefully, it wasn't the last time.

"I sure will, Joe."

After we hung up, I couldn't help but be pleasantly surprised by how Jalisa handled the news. I truly liked her, maybe even loved her. She was an amazing woman; I knew she would make a wonderful wife. It hasn't been long since we started messing around, but she made me feel different. Something that no other woman, not even Dareen, ever made me feel. But even with my feelings for Jalisa, I don't know if she truly felt the same. What if Dareen was truly pregnant? I would love to have a child, but not with her crazy ass. As a man, if it was mine, I would do what I needed to, but I truly prayed this girl was lying. I needed her out of my life permanently.

Chapter 26

Tommy & Dareen

I wanted to see Tommy after talking to Joe, but I needed some time to get my head straight. I was furious that he was sleeping around with that skank. The following day, I tried to meet up with Tommy, but he was too busy at work. So, instead, I gave him a call to tell him the news.

Ring ... ring ... ring ...

He answered the phone cheerfully and said, "Hey, beautiful. I hope you aren't mad, but we can't do lunch."

Without thinking twice about the delivery, I blurted out, "Tommy, I think I'm pregnant."

"Seriously? Oh, babe, that's awesome. I mean, I just started coming inside of you, and you're pregnant already." He was overjoyed and super ecstatic.

"I said I *might* be." I was trying to calm him down; I wasn't expecting that reaction from him.

"Well, we can go to the doctor and check it out. I'll start looking for one. Or do you have one?"

"Tommy, slow down, and let's just take this one day at a time," I insisted.

"Oh, babe, I'm excited. I hope we are. I guess this is how Eric felt," Tommy uttered, his voice getting high-pitched.

When I heard Tommy start talking about Eric, my heart skipped a beat, making my pussy throb as I reminisced on the other side of the phone.

"Monica? You there?" he asked, breaking me from my thoughts.

"Huh? Yeah, I'm still here," I replied, leaning back.

"Thought you hung up on me," he said while lowering his voice.

"Oh no, I'm here. I was looking at something. I'm sorry," I responded, completely distracted from our conversation. I finally arrived at Eric's home.

I was scoping out the neighborhood, getting ready to enter. "I can come by when you get off, OK?" I asked, trying to hurry off the phone.

"Monica, don't you think I should know more about you if you are pregnant? Meet your family, and you meet some of mine?" he asked.

"Can we talk about this later? I need to get some paperwork real quick." He aggravated my soul when he started that shit.

"Yeah, I guess. I just thought—" Tommy was about to say something crazy. I just knew it, so I cut him off.

"OK. Bye." I hung up so fast he couldn't get another word in if he tried.

After hanging up with him, I reached into my backseat for my gym bag. The neighborhood was quiet, and no one was at Eric's house. I removed my black leather gloves, lock pick, and mask from the duffle bag.

I placed the items on my lap as I moved my car farther down the street, where no one would notice. After scoping out their home a few times, I knew the street over had a little alley in between that would take me to the back of their home.

Taking my chances, I stuffed my items under my bra before leaving the car. I took a simple jog around the block, making sure the coast was clear. In my second lap around the neighborhood, I cut through the alley, finding the back porch entrance to their house.

Watching my step and checking my surroundings, I picked the lock quickly, sneaking inside. I hoped Eric would get home first so I could finally see my man.

I walked through their plush townhome. It seemed like the perfect household. Family photos lined the walls in their living room area. A cup of half-drunk coffee sat on the kitchen counter. I slowly walked up the stairs, which led me to the first upper level, which held another family area.

In the left corner of the wall was a picture of Eric with his red cap, gown, and Kappa pin, holding his diploma from NC State. I traced my fingers across his lips in the picture, thinking about how soft those lips felt on my body.

I took the picture from the wall, held it close to my chest, and whispered, "Oh, I missed you, baby. I can't wait to get you where you belong."

Putting the picture back on the wall, I went up the steps that led to the bedrooms. Their daughter's room was so pretty. They had painted the walls pink with yellow and white flowers. Her room smelled like lavender and baby powder.

After closing the door to her bedroom, I looked to my right and noticed another bedroom. It was *their* bedroom. I walked into the room, shut the door behind me, and then went over to their bed, observing how messy the sheets were. I removed my shoes and lay on their bed.

I sniffed the sheets, rolling around in them, thinking of how it would be to fuck Eric in those purple satin sheets. There was a stain on one of the pillows, and it smelled like coconut oil. As I lay there, I thought of how many times Eric and Reneece fucked in that bed instead of us.

I screamed all my frustrations into the pillow, hoping it would make me feel better, but it didn't. Immediately, I stood up and yanked all the sheets off the bed in a tantrum. I stood over the bed, breathing heavily. Finally, calming down, I looked to my left, noticing their closet.

I walked over to it and noticed a bottle of Gucci cologne at the top. I picked up the bottle and inhaled deeply, imagining Eric getting dressed in the morning, his scent lingering in the room and on his clothes. I couldn't wait to have that in person.

I eyed a little notepad at the top of the closet, grabbed it, took the pen from beside it, and wrote him a short note.

> *Dear Love,*
> *I survived the shot just like you. Don't you see we were meant to be? We will be together soon.*
> *Yours always,*
> *Dareen*

Then I sealed the note with a kiss and placed it on one of his bags at the bottom of his closet. Taking one last look at the bedroom, I walked out to leave before I got caught.

Tommy

I was excited that Monica might be pregnant. I always wanted to know what it felt like to be a father. Considering I was Hailey's godfather, I knew I would be awesome at it. I just couldn't understand why Monica didn't share my same excitement.

I wanted to see her, talk to her, and try to understand where her head was at. If she was pregnant, I wanted her to keep our child. It would be an amazing piece to add to our story. I hoped she understood that I loved her and wanted to be with her no matter what. I had some things in the office to handle before leaving for the day, so after my last meeting, I went to talk to Eric. I hoped my best friend could give me some advice.

I knocked on his office door, which he had left cracked open. "Yo."

"Aye, Tommy," he waved me in as he hung up the phone.

"I've got an answer from our painters, so we can get them in tomorrow to paint the club."

I was still perplexed about Monica, so I barely paid attention to the information he said. So, instead of having him repeat himself, I responded, "Cool. That's awesome."

"You a'ight, bro?" he responded, his eyebrow raised, questioning me.

"Nah, man . . . I think . . . I don't know." I tossed my hands over my head.

"Well, what's up? Close the door." I was happy that I was able to vent to him.

"Man, Monica is pregnant, and instead of being happy, she is acting like she just found out her life is over. I'm more excited than her. I don't get it. I love her," I exclaimed, pacing back and forth.

"Man, sit down and calm yo' ass down." Eric stood up, pointing to the brown leather chair in front of his desk. Once I sat in it, he shook his head. "Well, congrats, my dude. But you gonna force shorty to be distant if you pressure her."

"Yo, man, it feels like she's hiding something or someone. She just won't let me in." I was growing suspicious of her by the moment.

"Listen, if she is pregnant, deal with that first. She may have a lot on her mind," he advised while smiling down at his phone.

I waved my hand in front of him to regain his attention. "So, you're telling me to chill?"

"Yeah. Women become more emotional than usual when they're pregnant. Look, once we finish the club, we'll do a couples' night. We need to meet her anyway. We're family, and I gotta make sure you not just being played by a woman with some good kat." Eric joked with me, hoping to lighten my mood.

"Man, bro, I don't know about that." I was skeptical about that idea. I wanted her to be around them, my family, but she dodged every chance.

Eric leaned back in his desk chair and advised me. "Listen, I got you. Ease her into it. Don't force her. If it doesn't work, we'll come up with something else. Maybe pretend to take her out to eat. Then Reneece, Jalisa, her dude, and I will be there like a surprise type thing. I don't know, my nigga, but we'll work it out."

I agreed to let Eric help set up a couples' dinner with all of us. I assumed it would be cool. I was still unsure how she would feel about it, but I was willing to do anything to help her realize that her past was behind her and that I loved her. I left his office and texted her after she didn't answer my calls.

Me: Hey, Monica. Listen, baby, whatever you wanna do, I will support you. But you're not alone. I'm leaving work and want to see you. Come to the house. Let's talk, okay? I love you.

Chapter 27

Eric

I finally got home from a long, stressful day. Between meeting with the private eye, Detective Peterson, work, then Tommy's woman issues, a nigga was over the day. I walked into my home, and my wife had the house smelling good. She was cooking stewed chicken, sautéed carrots, wild rice, and honey corn bread. Just the smell of it made my stomach start talking to my back.

We sat in the dining room to have our dinner together. Hailey was up in her high chair, sucking on a chicken bone while we watched *Family Feud*. After dinner, we lounged around, letting our food digest. After doing the dishes, I went upstairs to watch ESPN. While watching TV, I realized it was getting late, so I decided to go for my nightly run.

"Babe," I yelled down the stairs, "I'm going for a run."

"OK, babe," she shouted from the edge of the stairs. "I'll finish cleaning up and bathe Hailey before you return."

I went to our bedroom to change into my black jogging pants, black and gray Nike hoodie, and Nike Tanjuns. I went to grab my gym bag to get my skullcap when I noticed a white piece of paper lying on top of the bag.

I assumed it was Reneece trying to do something sexy for a nigga, but when I opened it, I was horribly surprised. I read the note, and my blood began to boil when I saw her name.

I took the note with me, crumbling it into my pocket. I ran down the steps, kissed Reneece, and started my jog, playing my workout playlist. The more I ran, the more concerned and angrier I got. Like how the fuck did she know where I stayed, and how did she get into my house? I was so wrapped up in my thoughts I didn't even notice this silver car heading toward me until their lights blinded me.

I stopped in front of the stop sign on the corner and decided to call Detective Peterson.

"Hello, Detective Peterson," he answered the phone, sounding professional.

"Peterson, man, you got to help me," I said, breathing heavily.

"Help you? Eric? Eric, is that you?" he asked like he didn't recognize my voice.

Angry, I responded, "Of course, it's me. What the fuck is wrong with you? Did I call the wrong fucking person? Shit, man, there's some shit poppin' off, and you acting dumb."

"My screen got broken earlier at work in an altercation. I can answer but can't see who's calling. But, Eric, calm down and tell me what's going on," he said, waiting to hear me say something. "Hello? Eric, are you still there?"

"Yes, I'm here. I'm running and trying to find a place to stop." I jogged over to the playground area in my community and sat on a bench.

"Running for a workout or running from someone? What's going on? Are Hailey and Reneece OK? Talk to me," he shouted, almost bursting my eardrum.

"I came out for a jog. Man, that bitch was in my house!"

"Dareen?" he asked, sounding puzzled.

"Yeah, who else would I be upset about being in my shit?" I said, perplexed that he would ask me something so dumb.

Detective Peterson grew quiet. "Are you sure?"

"Dareen was in my fuckin' house! I'm fucking *sure* of it," I yelled at him.

"When? How do you know?" He was acting more like a police officer than a friend.

"Man, I don't fucking know. Man, like this shit is crazy, and you asking me stupid questions and shit." I felt as if I were being interrogated.

"Where are you? I can come meet you," he asked, trying to locate me, but I wanted to be alone.

"Man, I have to show her." I placed my face in my hands, screaming into them.

"Show Reneece? Show her what?" he asked.

"The ho left a note on top of my gym bag. Talking about she loves me and shit. *That's* how I know she was in my fucking house." I got up from the park bench and started my jog back toward my home.

"You want to show her that note? Now? We should wait. I'm telling you to wait. I'm asking you to wait. She doesn't need to know anything right now." He pleaded with me, but I wanted to be the man I was supposed to be for my wife.

"Yeah, man. I can't *not* tell her. The last time I held a secret, last year happened. So I'm telling my wife what the hell is going on," I explained, not wanting to hear any ands, ifs, or buts about it.

"Eric, I don't know if that's the wisest idea. I'm hoping we can find her and end all this madness once and for all." Detective Peterson was way too calm about this, which only upset me.

My voice grew stern and filled with aggravation. "Or *I* will end this. And I'm going to do it *my* way. I swear if she harms my wife or my daughter . . ."

"Eric, she won't—" He was about to tell me she won't hurt them, but that was bullshit.

Completely irritated with him, I cut off his statement. "You can't predict that. Look what happened last year. She even got into my house this time. How is that possible? You can't predict what she does." I was pacing back and forth as I raised my voice.

"Eric, this will not be a repeat, I promise. We *will* get her this time," he said confidently.

I began doubting his ability to help. "I'm going to head back to the house before my wife starts to worry. I'll hit you up tomorrow." I hung up the phone before he could say anything else.

After hanging up with the detective, I didn't feel he would handle it the best way possible. I was halfway down the street behind our home when I decided to call my private eye.

Answering on the last ring, he said, "Hey, Eric. I haven't called you yet because I don't have any leads. I didn't want to come to you with empty hands. You paid me to do a job, and that's what I will do."

"Fuck that. She been in my house. *Dareen has been in my house.* I will meet you at the gym where I work out at in the morning. I'll send you the time and address. I also need you to come up with a way to keep my family safe," I told him, catching my breath as I moved over to the side of the road.

"Say no more. I'll see you tomorrow. I'll start working on places for your wife and daughter. I'll try to find out Dareen's last whereabouts known that's not on police record," he said. I felt confident in choosing him to help me with this situation.

"Bet. I'll hit you up." I ended the call on my Bluetooth headphones as I turned back to the house.

All the way home, all I could think of was keeping my family safe. I jogged at a slower pace, trying to devise ways to tell Reneece about the note, Dareen, and my plan to get them out of town until I could get rid of Dareen for good.

I had said nothing since I came back in, and after my shower, I was lying in the bed with my towel when I heard Reneece come up the stairs with Hailey.

Hailey rushed into the room, giving me kisses. As always, Reneece and I took our daughter to her bedroom to put her to bed. We sat on both sides of the bed with her in the middle and took turns reading her favorite book, *Goodnight Moon,* as she dozed off to dreamland.

Then we crept out of her room so as not to wake her. I walked ahead of Reneece back to our bedroom, sat on the edge of the bed, and said nothing. I was really tense and frustrated. I knew my wife could sense it. She crawled on the bed with me, attempting to loosen me up, but my mind was elsewhere.

When she wrapped her arms around my neck and kissed it, I could tell she was in the mood, but I wasn't. She continued to caress my body when she finally asked me, "What's wrong, daddy? Tired from your run?"

"Nothing." I tried to dodge having this conversation, but I felt that she was about to make it hard for me to keep it in.

Reneece's hands traveled up my back under my shirt, and then she moaned slightly and said, "Something's wrong. It's all over you."

"We need to talk," I said as I sighed deeply, looking deeply into her eyes. Then I said one word: "Jalisa."

"What about Jalisa?" Reneece's chin sat on my right shoulder as she probed me.

I wanted to tell her, but then another part of me didn't. But I knew how keeping secrets can damage a relationship. Turning my head, I said, "When she said to you, 'Dude's girlfriend's name was Dareen.'"

"What about it? She's dead . . . Right? Eric, she's dead, *right?*" She stood up in the middle of the floor.

Lowering my head, I handed her the note. When I peeped to see if she was reading it, Reneece leaned against the wall. Her eyes filled with tears. I could only imagine what she was thinking or feeling . . . Everyone she lost because of Dareen . . . What we've recovered from over the past year . . . and her mom still barely hanging on to life . . . I knew she was going to be beyond upset knowing she was still alive.

"So, she really *is* still alive. Still coming for you? For us?" Reneece began to cry as she threw the note on the floor. I tried to console her.

"Reneece, she will never get to you or Hailey. I'm going to send you both away to make sure you're safe." I was trying to explain my plan when she cut me off.

Reneece got defensive as she came closer to me. "I'm *not* leaving and running like a little bitch. She's got the right one."

"Reneece, babe, I'm not asking. It's what you'll do," I told her, trying not to sound demanding.

"Eric, I'm not asking either. I ain't going no-fucking-where," Renecce said sternly, crossing her arms and rolling her neck.

"I'm trying to keep you both safe, don't you get that?" I questioned, trying to get Reneece to sit down.

"I'm not leaving," she said, looking me in the face. "Have you seen or fucked her lately?"

"Hell, fuck no. I'm just as surprised as you are that she's still alive. And still after me. I hoped she was dead just like you," I shouted at her as I sat on the bed.

"Well, not for long," Reneece stated as her cheeks got puffy and her breaths came faster.

"Babe, I got this," I reassured her, placing a smile on my face.

"No, *we* got this." Reneece stood over me with her fists balled up, ready to whoop someone's ass.

I didn't want to risk anything happening to her or Hailey. I couldn't have them at home while that crazy woman was on the loose. She was able to get into our home. My concern was my family above everything. No matter how hard I tried to plead and reason with her, Reneece wasn't going for it.

"As your wife, I took vows. And I'm sticking to my vows. Are you?" she questioned me.

Taking her hand in mines, I said to her, "I am. I just want you safe, away from all of this until I can resolve it."

"No, Eric." She kneeled, grabbed my hands, and looked at me with tears in her eyes. "Nobody's leaving. We'll be fine right here. This time, we find her, and we do everything *our* way. And we can call them once we know she's dead and won't come back to life," she stated, her puffy eyes filled with rage. She had every right to feel the way she did.

"Babe," I said calmly, hoping it would lower her tone.

"*No.* She will be twelve feet under by the time I'm done with her, and I put that on everything. Together, we do this and end her for good." Reneece stood up and walked into our daughter's room when Hailey started to cry. I was left sitting on our bed, trying to plot the best and next move.

Chapter 28

Joe & Dareen

Two Months Later

It was crazy to me that I was pregnant and not by who I wanted it to be. I told no one of this, not even my other two siblings whom I spoke to on and off. Yes, I have family, but I just don't deal with them. I am one out of a set of triplets. Our mother died giving birth to us, and our father did his best until a drug dealer murdered him for stealing his supply. We were about 16 years old when that happened.

After that, Lana, the "smart one," as my aunt Theresa would say, felt we needed to stick together and not be separated by the government. We moved in with Aunt Theresa and stayed there until one day, she took a real nasty fall. I hated that bitch. She always picked Lana or my other sister, Rebecca, over me for anything. She said it was 'cause I turned into a different person after we moved in with her. Maybe it was losing my parents, or maybe it was just me being a teenager, I don't know.

Our aunt fell to her death in a parking garage after she caught me fucking this guy I worked with. She was calling me all types of hoes and bitches. When I revealed to her I was pregnant, she slapped me and said, "I curse the day you were born, and your baby shall never have a decent mother in you."

I was so furious I pushed her, but I didn't know she was going to stumble, fall, and die. The guy was my alibi if I agreed to have an abortion. So, when I met Eric, he made me see men differently, and I fell in love with him. That's why I just can't let go.

But I digress. Tommy has been so involved with this pregnancy so far, but I didn't want him to get too attached. On the other hand, Joe has barely spoken two words to me. He was too busy finding a way to try to prove paternity before the baby was even here. If only he knew I didn't want the baby to be his or Tommy's.

It was early one Friday morning when I received a text from Joe.

Joe: Dareen, I want to meet you at Starbucks at Southpoint around 11:30.

Me: Why can't I just come downstairs? You shouldn't be treating me this way.

Joe: Meet me there, or you will only hear from me when it's time for the paternity test.

Me: Fine, Joseph, I'll meet you there.

I was going to give Joe his moment. I still needed him around and to be on his good side in case I had to run away if my plan went left.

I waited for him to arrive. While I waited, I ordered a hot chocolate from inside before sitting at one of their outside tables. I was drinking my hot cocoa when I got a text from Tommy. He was trying to get me to come over before I had to go to "work," but I was meeting with Joe. I told him I would come by during his lunch, and we could talk and stuff then. He was just doing the most about this pregnancy, but he was good about taking care of me. He kept my gas tank filled, money in my pockets, and we had good sex. He was texting me back-to-back.

Before I could finish texting him, Joe walked up to the table. He barely looked at me before sitting down.

"Let's make this quick. I got more important shit to do," he stated as he sat.

"Well, hi, Joe. A 'How are you?' would be nice. The fuck?" I replied, cupping my chin on my left fist.

Joe sucked his teeth at me. "Miss me with that 'you tryin'a make nice' bullshit."

"Joe, stop being an ass. You are being an asshole right now." I pointed out his attitude, but he couldn't care less.

He sat there looking at everyone but me and asked, "Is the baby healthy?"

"Yes, the baby is perfectly fine," I responded sharply, leaning back in the chair.

"Did you get an ultrasound?" he asked, putting on his Aviator shades.

Being short with him, I said, "Yeah."

"Let me see, Dareen." He had his hand out while looking around.

I threw the pictures of the ultrasound on the table and said, "There's your little bastard."

Joe got up and shook the table. Before he did or said anything, he looked me sternly in the eyes and said, "This child is not a bastard. Hopefully, it is *nothing* like you. And if the baby is mine, I'm taking you to court and taking my child away from you."

"Fuck you, Joe. You can have the little motherfucker. I don't give a shit," I shouted at him.

Joe threw his drink at me. "You're a piece of work, you know that? A shit-ass piece of a woman."

He turned his back on me, leaving me there to dry up his mess. I would go after him, but I didn't want to cause any bigger scene than what was already done. People were standing around, whispering and pointing their fingers at me.

"What the fuck y'all looking at? Mind y'all mother-fucking business, stupid-ass people," I screamed at the spectators while grabbing my things from the table.

I left Starbucks in a pissy mood. Since it was still early, I stopped by a school. I circled the block a few times before I decided to pull into the parking lot and park to have a better look.

Sitting in front of the school where Reneece worked, I watched her interact with the children. I was envious of her. I noticed how her body had changed over the past few months. I thought to myself, she couldn't be pregnant again. If that was the case, I was going to kill her *and* that baby. Eric didn't need any other kids with Reneece outside of Hailey.

I thought about how Eric and I could raise Hailey and how much Hailey would love me as her stepmother. I sat in my car, daydreaming of Eric and me and our future together. Our life would be perfect as long as Reneece stayed in her place. The more I watched her, the more I wanted to go up to her and cap one in her ass. But that wouldn't be the best move.

I pulled off from the school before I made a mistake. I was driving, listening to "Knock You Down" by Keri Hilson when I noticed this black car following me for a few minutes. It didn't matter how I turned, stopped, or what. They did the exact same thing. I wondered who it was and what they wanted. I intended to find out. I was belting my heart out as the song changed to "I Chose You" by Keyshia Cole. All I could think of was Eric. The car got closer to my bumper. I pulled into a McDonald's and waited to see what they would do.

The car pulled up beside me, blasting Lil Wayne's "No Ceilings" as he rolled down his window.

"Aye! Why you keep following me?" I shouted out of my window.

He just snickered. "My bad, ma, I thought you was someone I knew."

I threw up my middle finger at him. "Yeah, well, I'm not anyone you know, so fuck off, dude."

"OK . . . OK, just chill out. I'm not going to kidnap you or anything," he said, chuckling at my behavior.

"Once again, back the fuck off, or next time, I won't be this nice, OK?" I yelled at him, pretending to reach for a gun.

He nodded, then said, "Well, sorry to have scared you. Have a good day, miss."

The man rolled up his window and pulled off. I shook my head in disbelief. That guy had followed me for a long time. I had no clue who he was, but it was time for me to switch up things and tighten up my plan so my man and I could escape.

Stay In Touch

FACEBOOK:
Author Kandie Marie

Facebook Business Page:
@authorkandiemarie & @kmsweettreatsboutique

Instagram:
@authorkandiemarie

Twitter:
@authkandiemarie